I0672681

Kessum

The Crown of Glory

CHARNA AINSWORTH

The Crown of Glory

1Peter 5:4 And when the Chief Shepherd appears,
you will receive the crown of glory
that will never fade away.

Dedication: This one is for You.

Special Thanks to: My dad, Charles, my mom, Barbara, my husband, Greg, my daughter, Maria, and my friend, Amy McKay. Without your love and support, this book would have remained inside my heart.

PRELUDE

It was just a normal day, like all the others. I woke up, brushed my teeth, got dressed, and made breakfast. Nothing out of the ordinary or unusual happened. There were no strange feelings or thoughts entering my mind. It was just another day.

The regular morning routine fell out of sync when I spilled coffee on my white shirt. I rushed to change while the internal clock in my mind sounded the alarm to hurry, or I'd be late. There were thirty-six steps up and thirty-six steps down before I could be on my way to work. If I was going to be on time, I had to either hurry back upstairs or leave the phone.

Going upstairs was easy, other than catching my breath. With the keys still dangling in the lock, I searched without closing the door. It was on the arm of the couch, which was strange. Usually, I put the phone beside my keys on the kitchen counter.

The door closed harder than expected. Looking around, I checked to see if I'd disturbed anyone. That's when I noticed my next-door neighbor opening his door. Not wanting him to get in front of me, I quickly stepped back, twisting the knob, making sure it was locked. Rushing to be first, I barely said hello before beginning the 36-step descent.

The sound of my steps in fast repetition caused a strange echo in the stairwell. My neighbor called after me, asking why I was in such a big hurry. For a moment, I thought about pretending not to hear him. Wasn't it obvious I didn't have time to talk? How many mornings had he seen me rushing to get to work?

With one glance at my phone to check the time, my eyes lost sight of the next step. The phone flew out of my hand as the sound of flesh and bones hitting metal steps filled the stairwell. Everything began to move in slow motion. My body was falling, but somehow, I felt separate from it. There was a part of me that knew what was happening and another part that felt like it wasn't happening to me. Then, without another thought, my world faded into darkness.

CHAPTER ONE

For the first time in a long time, today felt like it would be a good day. After what happened yesterday, all I wanted was to have fun with my friends. We got on our group chat, and Cooley came up with the plan. They would skip school and spend the day with me on the lake. Trina and I volunteered to bring the things we'd need for lunch. We met down at Big Lake off Popp's Ferry Road. Shane Williams's family had a cabin, and his dad, Arthur, didn't care if we hung out there as long as we told him.

Shane Williams had it all: good looks, money, and popularity. He was the guy girls wanted to date, and the guys wanted him as their friend. In every way possible, Shane was his father's son. They looked alike, dressed alike, and their voices sounded similar. His Dad's reputation for drinking too much was well known, but everybody loved Mr. Williams. As far as the dads of Biloxi High teenagers, Shane's dad was the coolest.

There were seven of us—Cooley, Shane, Trina, Kelsy, Tommy, Sarah, and me. We hung out at the lake all day, and then Shane's dad came by later that evening to check on us. He brought two big bags of food from one of his restaurants. Arthur knew why we were hanging out, but he never asked me about what happened, which was good. I didn't feel comfortable talking about it with him. Besides, I didn't need another lecture.

When we finished eating, it was late, and everyone was tired. Trina and Kelsy planned to stay at my house anyway, so we decided to stay at the cabin instead. There was plenty of room for everyone to have a bed, but Shane, Cooley, and his dad stayed in the living room. Trina, Kelsy, and I slept in the master bedroom on the king-sized bed. Tommy and Sarah slept in the other two bedrooms.

Bright sunlight streaming through sheer curtains woke me up the next day. There wasn't any part of me that wanted to be awake. Thoughts of regret echoed in my mind as I turned on my side. I looked out the dirty windows, watching the breeze move the oak tree leaves. My thoughts wandered back to the principal's office and the things that were said. Then I thought about sitting on the couch, listening to my dad's words of disappointment.

Turning onto my back, I took a deep breath, trying not to think about it anymore or wake anybody up. My best friends, Kelsy and Trina, were still asleep with me in the middle. I didn't want to disturb them, but I had to go to the bathroom. Trina was on my left, and Kelsy was on the right. Not wanting to crawl over them, I rolled on my knees to stand in the bed, stepping over Kelsy.

Kelsy was the one I'd been friends with the longest. She asked me to be friends on the first day of the third grade. Back then, she had short, frizzy hair, thick, black-framed glasses, and was chubby. There were only a few people who wanted to be her friend, but I never cared what she looked like. All I cared about was whether she was nice. When I figured out she was not only nice but could keep a secret, we became best friends.

In a few years, her short, frizzy hair grew. Now, it was long, golden-brown curls that some girls who used to tease her wished they had. Her body slimmed up, and those ugly glasses were replaced with contacts, revealing beautiful, piercing blue eyes. Most of the time, Kelsy is a typical southern girl from Mississippi, sweet and quiet. But if you wanted a good morning, you didn't wake her up before she'd had her beauty sleep.

Trina, on the other hand, was an early bird. She woke up singing, full of energy, ready to start the day. She and I became friends in ninth grade because my dad and hers went to Biloxi High together. Our dads have known each other since third grade and graduated from high school one year apart. They were on the basketball and debate teams together. Although their history went back to grammar school, they never had a close friendship. Mine and Trina's friendship began during our third-period science class when we figured out that our dads knew each other. Something about the two of us clicked, and when she got along well with Kelsy, the three of us became inseparable.

None of us has much in common as far as looks are concerned. Where Kelsey is petite, beautiful, and quiet, Trina is tall, athletic, and outspoken. She is the only one in our group who has runway model looks. Her body is impossibly perfect. She has gorgeous blonde hair that falls in waves to her waist unless she has it in a ponytail, which is most of the time.

I knew Shane Williams personally for a couple of reasons. The first was that we'd been science lab partners in tenth grade for the first semester. The other reason is his best friend, Cooley. He was my first boyfriend in fifth grade, and we've been friends ever since.

Cooley had always been one of the cool kids, popular with every group on campus. As we grew older, he became something like a personal bodyguard to me. I couldn't count the times when Cooley protected me from bullies at school. Everyone was a little afraid of him because he's big, muscular, and looks a bit intimidating. Only people close to him knew that he was nothing more than a big teddy bear.

On my way to the bathroom, I looked out the window and noticed that the lake looked glassy—the trees along the water's edge, with white puffy clouds reflected on the surface. I wanted to go outside and experience the beauty I was seeing, but I didn't want to go alone.

Walking to the bathroom, I wondered how much longer everyone would sleep. Staring into the mirror, my eyes looked tired, so I decided to get back in bed. Gently, I crawled between my friends, pulling the covers up to my chin. The last thing I wanted to do was think about what had happened at school. No, it was better to relive what happened last night.

"Kessum, are you awake?" Trina asked.

"No, well, yes, but I don't want to be."

"Okay. Guess somebody woke up on the wrong side of the bed," Trina said, throwing back the covers.

"Sounds like you're the grouchy one."

She got halfway to the bathroom before asking, "Hey, what time are we supposed to be at work?"

"I don't even want to go to work," I said, lifting the covers to see if Kelsy was awake.

"Stop talking so loud!" Cooley yelled.

Kelsy, who was usually the quiet one, sat up, yelling, "You're such a butthead, Cooley!"

"Like he didn't already know that, Princess!" Shane yelled back, yawning loudly.

"It's like almost noon if this clock is right. We're scheduled to work from three to ten," Trina stated, closing the bathroom door.

The sun was shining brightly on this beautiful Saturday morning, and the lake was calling. It was also the day after the last day I'd ever have to be at Biloxi High School. Though I had cared about nearly everything for most of my life, today, I didn't care. I knew we would be late for work if I didn't go home to get ready. Thoughts of right and wrong swam in my head. Then, before I could think clearly, the words came out of my mouth. "I don't want to work anymore. I'm not going."

Shane sat on the edge of the couch, holding an empty glass up, cheering, "Here's to my girl, Kessum. She gave Biloxi High the boot one day and said adios muchachos to Taco Bell the next. She is as free as a bird!"

For a moment, I felt exactly like Shane said: free. No more responsibilities, no more early mornings, no more punching time clocks; I could do whatever I wanted. Then, my dad's voice was in my head again. Kessum, get up! You're going to be late! Don't you leave this house without making your bed! Kessum, what are you planning on doing with your life? Kessum, you have to have a job if you want to have money!

The voice that ruled my innermost thoughts was my dad's voice. It criticized everything I did wrong and everything I didn't do right. It was louder than mine almost all the time. That is, unless I was listening to music or partying with my friends.

Something had to change. It had to be me because Dad would never change. Neither would Mom, school, or my current job at the fast-food restaurant. They all wanted me to be something, be someone that just wasn't me. Instead of Kessum, the girl with real fears, real problems, they wanted a version of me that didn't exist. A girl who was always on time, dressed perfectly, and smelled like a rose. A girl who showed up early for school. She never spoke unless spoken to, and her name always appeared on the honor roll. A girl who came to work with a perpetual smile, working harder than everyone else for less money. That wasn't me, and it never would be.

When Trina said she was going home to get ready for work, I thought about crawling out of bed. Then Cooley came in, sat down, pulling the covers back.

"It's time to rise and shine, free-bird," Cooley said, handing me a bottle of water as I sat up. His brown eyes were full of life, but his black hair was a mess from sleeping on the couch.

Shane ran over, diving into the bed between Kelsy and me. My water sloshed out everywhere, but instead of yelling, I laughed.

Trina waved goodbye from the other side of the room before tossing her long blonde hair over her shoulder. Then, she closed the door a little too hard. We could tell she didn't want to work either. However, she knew she'd better go, or she'd have to face the consequences from her parents.

My dad would have plenty to say when he found out I quit my job, too. Mom probably wouldn't say much. She usually let me do whatever I wanted. She figured Dad had more than covered discipline for both of them. No, Mom never insisted on me being a certain way; instead, she expected me to know what she wanted. Sometimes, I liked it that way. Sometimes, I wish she would talk to me like an actual person, not a five-year-old child.

Cooley tickled me under the covers, asking, "Are you going to wake up?"

I pulled the covers over my head, and Shane forced them down, blowing in my face. Usually, that would have made me mad, but I smiled and blew right back.

"Oh my gosh, free girl. Get up and brush those pearly whites."

"Look who's talking," Kelsy said, turning her back to him.

Shane crawled over me, stopping to blow in my face again. He jumped down, almost running, like he was scared I would chase him. Then he stopped at the window, looking out toward the lake.

Tommy and Sarah walked into the bedroom holding hands. Tommy stood nearly a foot and a half taller than his girlfriend, which made holding hands a little awkward. His bright red hair and pale complexion didn't match her dark features. Sarah's family roots were Louisiana Cajun on both sides. And just like most people native to New Orleans, her hair is dark, with light brown skin and almond-colored eyes.

You might think Tommy and Sarah are an unlikely pair if you don't know them. However, in the teenage circles of Biloxi Beach, they were the couple everyone envied. In six years of dating, they only broke up once. It was during the summer between the ninth and tenth grades. Sarah's parents thought they were too serious at their age and forced the breakup.

During that time, Tommy liked another girl he met at summer camp from Mobile, Alabama. Her name was Angel, and even though they only kissed once, Sarah was still upset over it. To everyone who knew them, it seemed ridiculous for her to feel this way. In our eyes, none of the boys we knew ever loved a girl more than Tommy loved Sarah.

"Why are you two so happy?" Shane asked, turning toward Tommy and Sarah.

"It's a beautiful day. Let's have a party, dude." Tommy said, rushing up to Shane, finger-punching his chest.

"Dude, that freaking hurt. Not!" Shane yelled, grabbing Tommy's arm as they began playfighting.

Tommy winced in pain, calling, "Time out! Man, I didn't mean to wake the beast. You got to chill, dude. Where's your dad?"

"He went to get coffee or something. Said he'd be back later," Shane answered, grabbing Tommy's left arm while punching him in the right one.

Shane wasn't short or skinny, but his five-foot-eleven looked short compared to Tommy's six-foot-four lanky body. Tommy's big hand wrapped around Shane's head like a basketball, covering most of his wavy brown hair. Shane reached behind him, lifting Tommy's hand, and twisted to face him. Where Shane lacked in reach, he made up for it in muscle. With a couple of quick moves, he had Tommy's hand behind his back.

Kelsy threw back the covers, saying, "Could both of you little boys take yourselves out of our room?"

They stopped fighting, looked at each other, ran over to Kelsy, and bounced on the bed. She jumped up and ran to the bathroom, brown curls bouncing with each step. When she slammed the door, Tommy and Shane started laughing.

Sarah took Kelsy's spot on the bed. I sat up, looking at Sarah's eyes. Usually, they were a lighter brown, but today, they looked darker. I wondered if she was upset about something or still sleepy.

"The only way we're going to remember this day is if we do something worth remembering. We're young and free, so we don't have to do anything smart, just epic!" Cooley exclaimed.

"My thoughts exactly, dude. Let's make this a day we'll never forget!" Shane added, reaching out to Cooley, doing their special handshake.

By late afternoon, we had revived the little party we had started the day before. It didn't take much; it just took a few text messages, and people began to fill the cabin. By the time the sun went down, at least fifty people were hanging out with us. The music was loud, the place was packed, and everyone was having fun.

Sarah sat beside me, pushing her hair away from her face, asking, "Where's Tommy?"

"I don't know; I haven't seen him."

"I'm messed up," she said, leaning towards me.

"I think everybody is," I replied, leaning back so we didn't fall over.

"Hey, there's Shaaannee. Come here, Shanie," Sarah called, waving him over.

"There's my girls," he said, kneeling. "Do you know what this party needs?"

"Tommy?" Sarah asked.

Shane shook his head from side to side. "No, we have Tommy. We need fireworks! A bunch of loud fireworks. Something that'll wake up the whole neighborhood."

"Oh, but I like pretty ones with all that sparkly stuff. Can we do something like that?" Sarah asked, falling forward.

Shane gently moved her back, saying, "Wow! Somebody has had too much fun tonight. Kessum, where's Tommy?"

"We don't know. That's why we're asking you."

Shane looked to his left and right, searching for Tommy. "I'll go find him."

He walked toward the kitchen, and I moved Sarah toward the arm of the couch so I could help look for Tommy. There were so many people from school at the party. Almost everyone asked why I dropped out. I didn't know what to say, so I laughed or avoided the subject by asking if they'd seen Tommy.

As I searched the cabin, I noticed there wasn't a line for the bathroom. I went straight to the mirror, and it didn't lie. My makeup looked terrible, my hair was messy, and dark circles were under my eyes. I washed my hands, looking at my face again.

Taking some toilet paper, I wiped lipstick off my chin. Then I wet my hands and smoothed my hair down so it wouldn't look messy. I spotted some men's deodorant and dabbed some under my arms, then used mouthwash before looking at my reflection.

Somebody started banging on the door. They were saying something I couldn't understand, so I ignored them and used the bathroom. Looking out the small window, I could barely see the lake. A group of people were standing around a fire, so I figured Tommy must be one of them. One last look in the mirror, and then I opened the door to a long line of girls who didn't look happy.

When I walked by, I noticed Sarah was asleep on the arm of the couch. It wasn't like Tommy leaving her alone, especially at a party. He probably thought she was with me or Kelsy, but I didn't know where Kelsy was either.

When I was about halfway to the lake, I could tell it was mostly guys. I couldn't see if Tommy was one of them, which was odd because he's so tall. The thought crossed my mind to turn around and go back to the cabin. The guys were being loud and daring each other to do something, and it was probably something a girl didn't need to know about. If Sarah hadn't needed Tommy, I would have gone back inside.

As I walked down the hill toward the water, a loud blast suddenly made me stop in my tracks. The noise came from where the guys were, followed by cheering and laughing. At first, I thought Shane or one of his friends had found some fireworks. As I continued walking, I saw the barrel of a shotgun up in the air. A guy I'd only seen a few times was aiming it out over the water. When he pulled the trigger again, I knew it was most likely the shotgun I had seen earlier in the master bedroom.

"Tommy! Hey! Is Tommy down there?" I yelled, walking faster. The gun barrel was pointed straight up when the next shot blasted. I covered my ears, but it wasn't quick enough to keep them from ringing.

Someone was running up the hill toward me, but I didn't recognize who it was until he got closer. It was Cooley. He looked worried, so I asked what had happened.

"We need to get out of here," he said, taking my hand, pulling me towards him.

"I've got to find Tommy."

"Tommy is the one shooting the gun."

"I thought it was somebody else."

"Nope, it's him," Cooley replied, tugging my hand.

"Sarah is alone on the couch," I tried to explain as he kept pulling me up the hill.

"We gotta go!"

"Why? What happened?"

"Kessum, I'm leaving right now, and if you don't want to get in trouble, you better come with me."

"Why would I get in trouble? I haven't done anything."

"Do what you want to, but I'm not waiting around here for the police," he said, letting go of my hand.

For a moment, I watched him. Cooley didn't go inside. He went around the side of the cabin, disappearing into the darkness. I heard his truck engine start, but I didn't try to catch him. Instead, I ran toward the lake. Then I heard another gunshot followed by cheering. Way off in the distance, I could hear sirens. I heard Shane yelling, telling everybody to leave. It wasn't long before people started running in every direction. I felt confused because I wasn't sure where to go.

Shane rushed up to me, putting his arm around my shoulder. "I know where we can hide."

"Okay," I said, wishing I'd left with Cooley.

"Where's Sarah?" Tommy asked, handing Shane the shotgun.

I answered, "She's inside on the couch."

Shane pulled me towards him, "Come on, Kessum, it's this way."

We reached the back of the cabin, and Tommy went inside. Shane moved an old piece of wood and opened a little door. Then he said, "It's the storm shelter. There's a ladder going straight down. I can go first, but then you'd have to shut the door."

"I'll go first," I said.

We climbed down into the dark, musty storm shelter. When Shane closed the door, the darkness felt thick, like it might swallow me whole. He turned on his cell phone flashlight, and I stopped holding my breath. He took a flashlight off a shelf and handed it to me. I looked around, realizing it was nicer than it smelled. A twin-sized bed covered in plastic sat along one wall, and two metal chairs sat along the other. Shelves lined the other two walls, packed with survival gear and essentials.

Shane stood the shotgun in the corner and turned to me, putting his finger to his lips, asking, "Can you hear that?"

I didn't say anything, only nodded. We could hear cops yelling, telling everyone to stop. Shane looked up toward the door, and when he did, I noticed his shirt was dirty. He caught me staring, then pointed at the flashlight. I moved it until the light pointed down on the floor.

People kept calling his name. Shane stepped closer, whispering, "What should I do?"

Taking a step toward him, I leaned forward, whispering, "I don't know."

"I've never told you this, but you're so beautiful. I love your red hair," he whispered, leaning closer to my ear, touching my hair.

"It's strawberry blonde," I said, stepping back, staring into his green eyes.

"And those eyes," he sighed, "something about your brown eyes. So beautiful…"

"Everybody says I have my dad's eyes," I replied, feeling so nervous my body was shaking.

"You know Cooley still has a little crush on you, but did you know I've always wanted to kiss you?" He asked, stepping closer, then stared at me in the dim light.

"Do you think this is a good time to tell me?" I asked, my voice trembling.

"You had to know," he said, leaning forward, raising his hand to my neck.

"Maybe, but this isn't…"

"Just one kiss," he said softly, pressing his lips to mine. Then he looked up at the ladder and said, "Guess I better face the music." I don't want anybody else to get in trouble over this. Hey, if you stay down here until everything is quiet, you'll be okay."

"If I can stay by myself that long. I'm scared of the dark."

"Me too, Kessum, but I'm not as afraid of the dark as I am of opening that door."

He leaned toward me, wrapping his arms around me. I thought he changed his mind because he didn't let go. Finally, he stepped back, reached out for the ladder, and slowly climbed up. He looked down before he opened the door, but I could barely see his face.

"Here he is," the policeman yelled.

"I'm Shane," he said, quickly climbing out and closing the door.

"Anyone else down there?"

"Nope, just me."

"Move to the side and get on your knees. Put your hands behind your head. Do you have any weapons?"

I could hear Shane answer as the door to the storm shelter opened. I moved over into the corner closest to the stairs. When a bright light hit my face, I looked down.

"One female. You need to climb on up here," the officer said, keeping the light on me.

With each rung, it felt as though gravity were increasing. There was nowhere to go and nowhere to hide. The bright light flooded my eyes, affecting my vision. As soon as it adjusted to the darkness, I saw Shane sitting alone on the backsteps. He had handcuffs around his wrists and a frown on his face. Somebody I didn't know stood beside him, telling a police officer it was Shane's house, his party, and his gun. Shane didn't say anything; he didn't even try to defend himself.

"It's his daddy's cabin, but it wasn't his party. It was my party. I'm the one who wanted to have it," I said, wishing I could suck the words back into my mouth.

"Is this true?" The policeman asked.

"No, she's just trying to protect me," Shane said, looking at me, moving his head from side to side.

Something inside me began to boil with anger. Why were the cops even at our party? What had we done to hurt anyone? We're just a bunch of kids wanting to have fun.

"He's telling the truth, officer. Kessum didn't have anything to do with it," Tommy interjected.

What's wrong with both of you? I'm the one who dropped out of high school, quit my job, and didn't want to go home. That's why we're having this party!

"In that case, you are under arrest. Put her in cuffs and put her in the back seat beside her little boyfriend, Shane Williams. His dad should be here any minute."

The sound of the car door shutting with my hands cuffed behind my back felt unreal. Blue light bounced back from nearby surfaces, filling my eyes. Emotionally, I felt numb. I was neither sad nor angry. Shane scooted closer, trying to console me. I looked out the window, not answering his questions. The moment felt surreal, and I wasn't truly processing what was happening.

Suddenly, the car door opened, and a policeman took Shane by the arm, helping him out of the backseat. He was telling me not to worry. He said his dad would help as they slammed the door shut. Sitting alone in the police car, the silence enveloped me as tears fell down my cheeks onto my blouse. How could so many bad, horrible things happen to me in such a short amount of time?

The next morning, Mom stared at me through the thick glass of the jail. Her hazel eyes looked tired, and her brown hair was messy. When they opened the lock on the heavy door, it swung open. She turned to speak with a man behind the counter. He handed me my stuff in a brown envelope. She never said anything to me, barely looking my way. I followed her down the steps, noticing she looked thin. Walking to the parking lot, I realized I was at least an inch taller than Mom. I was wondering when that happened, as she unlocked the passenger door. I sat in the seat, waiting for her to speak, but she never said a word all the way home.

We walked into the house, and Dad was sitting on the couch, folding a newspaper. He stared at me, and I realized he was no longer a young man. His reddish-brown hair was thinning, and he had wrinkles around his eyes. Those sad brown eyes spoke volumes. He was worried, hurt, and angry. I wanted to ignore him and the advice he began giving generously. I thought about telling both of them I was sorry. I wanted to hug my parents and promise never to do it again. Instead, I sat quietly and for the first time in my life, saw my parents as just people. I saw them as - Pam and Richard.

There were things I had to do if I still wanted a roof over my head. There were things I couldn't do if I wanted to eat for free at his house. A list of people I couldn't be around, including Shane Williams. Who, if I didn't know, didn't even spend the night in jail because of his Daddy. Another list of places I had to be and an even longer list of places I couldn't be at if I liked sleeping in a warm bed. And if I enjoyed taking hot showers, there was a long list of chores I had to do every day.

In just a few short hours, I had gone from a senior in high school working part-time on my way to college to what felt like a prisoner in my own home. No phones, computers, or tablets were allowed. I could watch one hour of television at night, but only if I finished my chores. Dad decided that if I wasn't in high school or going out with friends, there was no reason to have a job or make money.

For months, I spent every day and night with Mom and Dad. I cooked, cleaned the house, and washed clothes. On weekends, I helped Dad keep everything running smoothly inside and outside the house. I woke up at 6, started working at 7:00 a.m., stopped at 7:00 p.m., and went to bed at 9:00 p.m. My life had become a schedule, void of pleasure or social interaction. It was my punishment for disappointing the people who gave me life.

In a way, I felt I deserved to be nothing more than a servant to my parents. They said I owed them, especially Dad. They sacrificed their wants and desires so I could have a good life. They wanted me to have the things they never had when they were growing up. All they required was to go to school, get good grades, go to college, and get a degree. However, I didn't even manage to earn a high school diploma. On top of that, I quit my job and got arrested.

The crushing feeling of failure consumed me as each day of isolation passed. I began to feel more desperate to make something of my life. Many thoughts entered my mind when I got into bed at night. Some made me feel like what my parents were doing was justified because my actions deserved consequences. Other times, all I could think about was the last night I saw Shane Williams and the kiss we shared.

Late one night, my thoughts became overwhelming. The air in my bedroom felt thick, making it hard to breathe. I couldn't sleep, and I couldn't take it anymore. If this was all life had to offer, I was done.

In the heat of the moment, I stuffed my backpack full of everything I thought was important. Then I put what little money I had in the zipper pocket on the front. Whatever clothes and shoes I could fit went in a gym bag, and then I threw it out the window. With one last look around the bedroom, I climbed out, feeling like I might never see this place again.

Once my feet touched the dew-soaked grass, I felt like I had been holding my breath for months. I took a deep breath, filling my lungs with the cool night air. There were choices to be made, but my thoughts were jumbled from the adrenaline rush of climbing out the window.

My initial plan was to walk until I decided what to do. After all, I could do several different things to change my situation. First, I needed to clear my mind and decide on my next move. Whatever it was, I knew it would send me in one direction or the exact opposite. My mind raced with possibilities. Faces of friends and familiar places flashed in my memories. Without a doubt, I knew the most important thing to do was to leave my parents' house. It wasn't easy, but I kept walking, never looking back.

CHAPTER TWO

Distant streetlights barely lit the rough-paved road that led to freedom. All I kept thinking was just put one foot in front of the other. Take one step at a time. Those simple words, repeated over and over, helped me reach the entrance of my subdivision. To the right were the lights of Biloxi, Mississippi. They hung low in the sky, encased in a foggy mist. It was much darker to the left, but that was the direction I needed to go. Kelsey didn't live far away, and getting there wouldn't take long. Even though I was afraid of the dark, I started repeating one step at a time, walking faster.

Thoughts of doubt interrupted my cadence every so often. I pushed them back, reminding myself I'd have plenty of time to think once I reached Kelsy's house. There was no denying I'd made a few bad choices. The truth was my parents had also made choices. Keeping me on an indefinite lockdown wasn't the solution to our problems. Still, even as I walked down a dark highway, I wondered if I had made the right choice by leaving.

Finally, after walking for about an hour, I stood in front of Kelsy's house. The window to her bedroom was on the left side of the house. I looked around to see if anybody was watching but didn't see anyone.

Before I knocked on Kelsy's window, I knew she was still awake because her light was on. She came to the window, barely pulling back the curtain. She jumped up and down when she saw my face. She struggled to open the window, so I pushed while she pulled. With the window half open, I handed her my things, then she helped me crawl inside.

We were still on the floor when she hugged me, asking, "Where have you been?"

"At home. Where did you think I was?"

"Oh my gosh! They've been lying to us."

"What do you mean?" I asked, standing up.

"After you were arrested, everybody tried to see you. Your mom and dad said you were sick, and they were getting you the help you needed. They said you went to a camp for teenagers who get in trouble."

"No, I've been there with them. I was beginning to think nobody cared about me."

"That's crazy. Why didn't you call me?"

"They wouldn't let me, and then I just couldn't take it anymore, so I left."

"It's okay. I'm glad you're here," she replied, standing up to hug.

I released her embrace, picked up my bag and backpack, put them in the corner, and pulled a tissue out of the box. "Is it okay if I stay with you tonight?"

"Sure, but I probably should tell my mom."

"I don't know. My parents are going to figure out that I left. Maybe I should go somewhere else."

"No, you're not leaving, not after I haven't seen you in like forever. We'll figure it out. Everybody's been worried about you, including my mom. We had no idea what happened."

"Nothing happened except they cut me off from the world. I know they want to protect me, but…"

"Yeah, but they flipped out because you got arrested."

"I know," I said, sitting on the edge of the bed.

Kelsy sat beside me, saying, "You are eighteen. You don't have to live there anymore."

"That is correct, but where am I going to live? What am I going to do?"

We lay in bed talking into the early hours of the morning. Kelsey's Mom woke us up around nine. My parents had already called, looking for me. I explained the situation and that my parents might send me somewhere I didn't want to go. Then I told her mom I wouldn't be here long. She agreed to let me stay. However, I had certain things I had to do. The first was to let my parents know I was okay and tell them why I left.

When I called, Mom answered. She said Dad was out looking for me. I apologized for leaving without saying goodbye, explained where I was, and that I wouldn't be coming back. She didn't have much to say, which was what I expected. She asked me to come back. She promised things would be different. I told her I needed a few days to think, but I knew I was never going back home.

Within the first few days of living at Kelsy's house, I fell into the rhythm of her family's daily routine. It was easy for me to cook, clean, and help around the house. Her parents quickly became less concerned about how they could care for another person and became thankful because I made their lives easier.

Word spread quickly around town that I was staying with Kelsy. It wasn't long before we were invited to a party. After living without my friends, I couldn't wait to see a few familiar faces. It had been too long since I'd had fun. The only bad thing was that Kelsy wouldn't tell me whose party it was or where it would be. She said she wanted it to be a surprise.

We tried on half of her clothes and most of mine before we found the right outfits. Kelsy had on a white cotton summer dress with wedge heels. I wore a black miniskirt, a silky white shirt, and black heels. Kelsy had been doing my hair and make-up since we were kids, so I agreed to let her do it again. When we were ready, we both stood in front of the mirror like we'd done so many times before. Something was different about both of us this time. Maybe it was because we were growing up, or maybe it was something I could only feel, not understand.

We hopped in her car, but she still wouldn't tell me where we were going. As we turned into the neighborhood, a flood of memories hit. Part of those memories was like returning to the scene of a crime. The sound of gunfire filled my mind, and the moment before the trouble started, Cooley asked me to leave with him. The strange smell of a storm shelter and Shane's lips pressed against mine. Then the memory of blinding blue lights and how it felt to sit handcuffed in the back seat of a police car.

"Kessum, are you mad?" Kelsy asked, turning off the ignition.

Without an answer, I opened the passenger door. Each step I took toward the cabin made my heart flutter with excitement. He was here, and it would only be a matter of minutes before we looked into each other's eyes. Did he think about me the way I'd thought about him these past few weeks? It was only a kiss shared in secret while we hid from trouble. It was one of the best moments of my life, but I didn't know if he felt the same.

Shane sat in the middle of a small group, talking about somebody falling off his boat. He had everyone's attention, as usual. I'd forgotten how charismatic he became when telling a story. It was hard to ignore him when he spoke with passion about what he was saying. All eyes were glued to him, hanging on every word.

Cara, a girl from Gulfport, was practically sitting in his lap on the couch. She stared up at him, giving every emotion expected, cued by the crowd. I watched them, standing near the island in the kitchen. Shane was exactly like every memory I'd played on repeat in my mind. Handsome, well-dressed, perfectly comfortable in his skin, and popular. We were complete opposites, and I suddenly felt foolish for thinking about him so much.

Shane stood up, showing everyone how his friend fell from the bow while throwing the anchor. Cara reached for his hand and pulled him back down to the couch. He kept talking, but then he leaned over and kissed her cheek. I watched as he didn't let go of her hand.

"Kessum!"

"Cooley, I hoped I'd see you here."

He ran, picked me up, spun me around, and said, "I missed you, girl. Where have you been? What happened?"

"My parents put me on lockdown," I answered, still in his arms.

"It's good to see you," he replied, gently letting go until my feet were back on the floor. He smiled, looking into my eyes, then put his arm around my shoulder.

"Me too, I had to get out of that place," I said, catching Shane's eyes. He let go of Cara's hand and walked over.

Shane hugged me, saying, "I thought you were going to that camp in Hattiesburg."

"No, I'm still here."

"This is the girl who got arrested?" Cara asked, taking Shane's hand, standing close to him.

Cooley stepped forward, saying, "Hey, Kessum, let's go to the lake. Tommy and Sarah are down there."

"Sure," I answered, taking his hand.

We walked through the house with every eye turning to look. It had never crossed my mind that I'd have a reputation for getting in trouble one day. It wasn't in my nature since I always tried to be a good girl who followed directions.

Even though she promised, Kelsy rarely stayed by my side at a party. She was quiet and sweet but tended to be more of a social butterfly in large groups. There were a lot of people from school and a few new faces in the crowd. Thankfully, Cooley stayed by my side. Of course, I thought about him when I was stuck at home, but I didn't realize how much I'd missed him. Cooley had a way of making me feel comfortable. When I was with him, I could relax and not worry about a thing.

My excitement about seeing Shane drifted away when I realized he was with Cara. Why I thought someone like him would be sitting around thinking about me seemed ridiculous now. He was Shane Williams, one of the hottest guys from Biloxi, and entirely out of my league. Our kiss was probably one of a thousand for him. He had no way of knowing it was the best kiss of my life.

Hours passed like minutes, and before I knew it, it was time for us to go home. Kelsy didn't want to drive, so she handed me the keys. After we pulled into her driveway, I told Kelsy I'd come inside in a few minutes. She was tired and didn't argue. She picked up her purse, we hugged, then she walked toward the front door. I turned the key in the ignition so the radio would play. After switching channels a few times, I finally heard a song

I liked, A Sky Full of Stars, by Coldplay. I sang, putting the window down to look at the sky.

"There's a bunch of stars out tonight."

"Shane, you scared the crap out of me!" I said, grabbing his arm.

"You can sing, girl. Don't stop because of me," he said, moving until his hand held mine.

"I'm not about to sing for you, if that's what you're thinking," I replied, turning the key.

"You didn't have to turn it off; we could've danced," he said, letting go of my hand.

"What are you doing here?"

"I didn't get a chance to talk to you earlier."

"Uhm, because of your girlfriend," I said, under my breath, getting out of the car.

"Well, she's more like a friend who's a girl."

"I don't think Cara would feel that way," I said, looking toward the house.

"Can't we just talk?" He asked, turning to stand in front of me.

"Where's your girlfriend?"

"I took her home," he answered, stepping forward.

"That was fast."

"Kessum, I broke at least seven laws to get here before you went inside," he almost whispered, touching my cheek.

"What are you doing, Shane?"

"I'm going to kiss you, if you'll let me," he replied, leaning toward me until his face was only inches away from mine.

"What are you waiting for?"

We kissed the kind of kiss every girl dreams about. It was soft, sweet, and full of passion. With my eyes closed, I thought of how many times I'd imagined this moment. Then I realized it exceeded all my expectations.

He pulled me closer and hugged me harder than anyone had ever hugged me. While he held me tightly, I knew there was no hope for me. There was no way of protecting my integrity or dignity. I was putty in his hands. From this moment forward, I knew my life would never be the same again.

"Where have you been, pretty girl?" He asked, pushing hair away from my cheek.

"Not far."

He leaned back, looking at me, and said, "It was like you fell off the face of the Earth."

"No, I'm still here," I smiled, stepping back.

"Man, what's your parents' problem?"

"After I took a ride in that cop car, they put me on lockdown."

He took a step back, and so did I. Shane shook his head, looked down at the concrete, then took another step back. It was something I wasn't prepared for in my fragile state of mind. Without even thinking, I clicked the lock button on the key fob and turned to walk inside.

"Hey, where you going, pretty girl?"

"I'm going to bed."

"Don't cry, Kessum," he said, rushing to catch up to me.

"I'm sorry, I don't understand why you're here."

He reached for my hand, pulling me around to face him. Reaching up, he wiped the tear falling down my cheek. Forcing myself to stop crying wasn't working, so I forced a smile instead.

"I'm here because I missed you. That should be obvious," he replied, taking my other hand.

"You and I, we don't, we can't. I mean, we're from two different worlds. And you got a girlfriend. This is not, I mean you're not just trying to…"

"No, I'm not trying to do anything. And you can say we're from two different worlds, but as far back as I can remember, we've lived in the same town, went to the same school."

"Shane, you know we don't belong together. You have everything: money, a car, a great family, and a future. I have nothing: no money, no car, no future. Do you realize I'm homeless? I have three hundred and forty-seven dollars to my name, no job, no income, and no diploma. I don't know what I'll do when Kelsy's parents tell me it's time for me to go. One thing I do know… I'm never going back to live with my parents!"

"You are so beautiful when you get upset," he said softly.

"Do you think kissing is going to solve my problems?"

"Maybe. At least it calmed you down a little bit."

When Shane pulled me close, holding me in his arms, tears began to travel from my eyes onto his perfectly ironed blue shirt. He saw my tears, then pulled me even closer. His kisses made me feel warm, but my uncertain future filled me with fear.

"You're in luck, pretty girl," he whispered in a deep voice. "I just so happen to be great at problem-solving. What do you think about going to my house? We could talk about it and figure out what to do."

"Let's go!"

We walked down the driveway to his car. He opened the passenger door, waiting for me to get in before he closed it. He pushed the ignition, and the engine turned over. It sounded more like a racecar than a sports car. Shane put the car in drive, reached over to hold my hand, and slowly drove away.

When we arrived, he drove through the grass and parked behind the house. He opened my door, reaching for my hand, helping me out of the car. Shane reached over the tall fence surrounding the back of the house, pushing something to unlock the gate. The door swung open to a dimly lit, beautifully landscaped backyard with a pool.

Walking hand in hand, we crossed almost the entire length of the backyard. There was another small house, which had nothing but windows on the front. When we got closer, Shane ducked, and I followed, but it was too late. There was a motion-sensor spotlight, and we triggered it. An enormous amount of light flooded the backyard as we rushed through the door.

"Welcome to our pool house," he said, flipping a switch to turn off the spotlight. He closed the door, stumbling in the dark to turn on a lamp.

"Thank you. It's so nice."

"Come sit with me."

Shane walked around an oversized sectional couch, sitting in the middle, patting the cushion beside him. He reached for a remote-control, turned-on music, and lowered the volume.

My mind was going in ten different directions at once. I had so many thoughts at the same time, it was hard to act normal. This was one of those times when I shouldn't be confused. It was one of those times I needed to have my thoughts together. I was at a boy's house, not just any boy, and we were alone in his pool house. I needed to make good choices, and my mind needed to be clear to do it. With one deep breath, I walked around the massive couch and sat beside him.

"Okay, let's figure this out. Tell me what you need."

"Shane, I know you want to help, but I can't ask you to do that."

"You're not asking me, Kessum. I'm asking you. There's a difference."

"I know, but I need to figure this out on my own."

"What did you say earlier, a place to stay, and a job?"

"Yes, but I mean, I have a place to stay right now. I have a little bit of money, but it's not enough to get my own place."

"Dad owns a bunch of apartments. I know he'd be willing to help you out."

"I don't want you to ask Mr. Arthur. He probably doesn't even like me after what happened at the cabin," I replied, standing up.

"Don't get stressed out again. Sit down, relax."

"Shane, I'm sorry, but I think I'm ready to go back to Kelsy's house. If her parents wake up and realize I'm not there, then I might not be able to stay."

"It's no problem. I'll take you back."

"Thanks, I hope you're not mad."

"No, I'm not mad, Kessum."

We drove through the stillness of the night in silence. He didn't hold my hand, like he did on the way to his house. Tears kept filling my eyes, but I never let them fall. I looked out the passenger window, silently asking myself what's wrong with me.

I had been asking God to help me for months. Now I wondered if the help Shane offered was the answer to my prayers.

He pulled up along the end of the driveway and put the car in park. He left the engine running and got out to open my door. I stepped out, and Shane put his arms around me, hugging me gently, and then closed the passenger door.

"Thanks for bringing me back."

"No problem. I hope you'll think about what I told you. Just sleep on it," he whispered, stepping back.

"I know you want to help, but…"

"Everybody needs help sometimes. Don't think you'd owe me anything; I'd never expect payback, not even a kiss," he said softly, with sadness barely hidden by words.

"I know you wouldn't. Now… I see you differently, Shane Williams. Behind your tough exterior, you have a big heart."

"That's why I like you so much, Kessum Howards; you're real. Nothing fake about you, like most of the girls I know."

"I don't know what to say…"

He took my hand, looked in my eyes, suggesting, "How about see you tomorrow?"

"See you tomorrow."

He let go of my hand. I took a few steps back. He stepped forward. I stopped. Then he winked, and I smiled, turning to walk to Kelsy's window. It wasn't until I crawled inside that I heard his car drive away.

Kesly and I woke up the next day to dozens of text messages on her phone. All of them were from friends, but only one was from Shane. He asked if I was mad at him or if everything was okay. All the other messages were from our friends who wanted to meet on Biloxi Beach.

Biloxi Beach was packed with locals and tourists. Our friends were close to the pavilion across the street from the Coast Coliseum. When I didn't see Shane, I wondered what had happened. I asked to see Kelsy's phone, then heard somebody yelling my name.

"Who's that guy out there, Kelsy?" I asked, pointing toward the boat.

"That's Cooley," she said, raising her arms.

"Oh, now I see. Duh!"

"Hey, Shane sent a message," Kelsy said, handing me the phone.

Shane asked us to meet them at Biloxi Harbor. On the way back to the car, we saw Tommy and Sarah and invited them to go with us. We packed their things and walked back up the beach toward Highway 90. We got in Kelsy's car, turned up the radio, and we all sang together on the way over to meet them.

Shane stood at the end of the pier, waving for us to come. Tommy ran, pulling Sarah along. Kelsy was carrying her beach bag and had a backpack on, so the most she could do was jog. I stayed with her, beach bag in one hand and a small ice chest in the other.

Shane fist-bumped Tommy, turned to help Sarah onboard, then ran to help us. He took the ice chest, saying hello, barely touching his lips to my cheek. My heart felt like it fell to my feet when our eyes met. He turned to take Kelsy's beach bag and ran back to the boat. By the time we reached the end of the pier, Shane was holding out his hand to help us board.

It was just the six of us, though some of Shane and Cooley's neighborhood buddies were out on their boats, too. We went to

Horn Island first, then Ship, and then Cat. We laughed, swam in the clear waters beyond the barrier islands, and no one talked about the future. We were fully immersed in the moment, the here and now.

At nearly sunset, everyone left Cat Island. Then, with the sun on our backs, we slowly cruised until we reached the middle of Ship Island. There we anchored, jumped in the water, and walked ashore.

Shane laid a blanket down, barely giving the six of us enough room to stay out of the sand. He sat close behind me, and for a moment, I imagined leaning back to rest in his arms. With a deep breath, I pushed the thought away and sat quietly watching the sun set.

Shane leaned up, whispering, "Hey."

"Hey," I said, turning my head slightly toward him.

"Want to go for a walk?"

"Sure."

He stood, pulling me up, but didn't let go of my hand. Kelsy looked at me, smiled, and quickly turned her attention back to the setting sun. Then Cooley turned around, looked us up and down, and stood to his feet.

"Where are ya'll going?" Cooley asked.

Shane let go of my hand, answering, "We were just going to walk down the beach to talk."

"I guess that's a private conversation," Cooley half asked, but mostly stated, still staring at us.

Shane looked at me, then answered, "Only if Kessum wants it to be."

"Maybe it should be," I said, looking over my shoulder at Shane.

Cooley walked away in the opposite direction. It wasn't easy to stop myself from going after him. He had always been so good to me, and the last thing I wanted to do was upset him. At the same time, I had to talk to Shane. After last night, I needed to find out what he was thinking.

Shane didn't say anything, and neither did I. We walked along the water's edge, toward the sun. The tension I'd read about in books was there between us. It was an unseen force drawing me to touch him. It was all I could think about, and I wondered if Shane felt it, too.

When there was distance between us and our friends, he reached over, touching my fingers with his. I felt energy travel from Shane's fingertips into my hand, up my arm, and straight to my heart. Our fingers interlaced as we walked toward the island's western shore, as the sun sank closer to the water.

"Did you think about what I said last night?"

"Yes, I did, Shane."

"You still won't let me help you?"

"No, I can't let you do that."

"Why, Kessum?"

"Because I don't want to be your charity case."

"It wouldn't be like that," he said, squeezing my hand.

"You say that now, but…"

"There's no but in this situation. Erase it from your mind."

"Thanks, but…I don't know what else to say," I replied, letting go of his hand, looking out toward the Gulf.

"Let me help you."

"You know, Shane, I thought I knew the type of guy you are, but I didn't."

"Me… being misunderstood, it's more common than you know."

"In reality, no one truly knows who anyone is deep inside. The truth is, sometimes we don't even fully know ourselves. Under the right circumstances, we might be surprised how we'd react."

He stopped walking, turned to face me, and said, "You are so beautiful, Kessum. I never thought you'd give me a chance."

"What are you talking about, Shane? I thought you'd never even look at me twice."

"I'm looking at you right now," he spoke softly.

In a dreamlike haze, his hand gently touched my cheek. Feeling his skin upon mine was like a drug. There was no way to resist it. The craving for his touch and the sound of his voice was unlike anything else I'd ever felt in my life. I closed my eyes as familiar lips touched mine. Then my heart felt like it expanded as butterflies danced in my stomach.

Could this moment have been written in the stars before he and I were born? All I knew was whatever fears had bound me, and every bit of nervousness I'd been feeling left as we stood on the beach kissing. My mind went blank, and if I was thinking about anything, it was that I never wanted this moment to end.

"There's something about you. I don't know. There are so many girls around me, but I can't stop thinking about you, Kessum."

"If this is just another hook up for you, please don't. My heart isn't strong enough…"

"It's not a hook up. I've never felt like this. Now I sound like one of those stupid rom-com movies."

"No, you don't, Shane. You sound like a boy standing on a beach with a girl, telling her how he feels."

"Let's do this, you and me. Me and you, I don't care what they say. I want to be with you."

I whispered, "I can't stop thinking about you either. I don't know what happened in that storm shelter, but from that moment..."

"It was that first kiss," he said, picking me up, spinning me around. "Ever since that moment, even when I've kissed other girls, all I could see was your face. It's so messed up, but I can't stop it."

"What are we going to do, Shane?"

"Do you want to be with me?"

"Yes, but..."

"Don't," he said, taking both of my hands. "It's either yes or no. Look, I don't know what I'm doing either."

"Okay."

"Okay, if you're my girl, you have to let me help you."

"Okay."

"I'll talk to my parents. Getting an apartment and a job shouldn't be a big deal. They own three complexes and four restaurants."

"Thank you, Shane. I promise I'll work hard to pay you back."

"There's no payback between us, not now, not ever."

He stared into my eyes, as if he were searching for an answer without words. Our eyes locked, but we didn't say anything. In my mind's eye, I began to see a future that I could never have imagined before we kissed. Something in the way Shane spoke, in the way he touched me. It made me feel like a different person. If I could trust and completely love him with all my heart, I felt like we could stay together forever.

Feeling so lost while looking into his green eyes, I told him, "I won't let you down."

"Then I'll never let you go," he replied, kissing me one last time before we began to walk back.

CHAPTER THREE

The wind blew the rain sideways, tapping against the cabin windows. Something about being near the lake made storms seem more intense. Lightning crashed nearby, sending me diving under the covers. I counted one Mississippi, two Mississippi, three Mississippi, then thunder rolled on and on. For a moment, I thought about Mom and Dad. Weeks had passed since we last spoke. The way things ended between us was the catalyst, the fuel that kept me going even when I didn't know what to do. The one thing I did know was that I was never going back home. Somehow, some way, I was going to make it in this world, with or without their help.

Shane's parents, Annie and Arthur, took me in when I had nowhere to live. They let me stay in their cabin on Big Lake. They didn't ask me to pay rent. Instead, they asked me to open a savings account for my future. I also got a job as a server at one of their restaurants. It wasn't the easiest work, but most of the time I made decent money.

Annie Williams was the most glamorous woman I'd ever spent time with. When she was younger, pursuing a career in modeling, she graced the covers of several local magazines. She still had the look: tall and slender, with gorgeous green eyes and perfectly styled golden-brown hair.

As the storm moved farther inland, I didn't feel as scared. I pulled the covers down but stayed in bed. A few minutes later, I could only hear the sound of thunder in the distance. With a loud yawn and a long stretch, my feet hit the floor.

The bathroom mirror told a story I didn't want to hear. Splashing water on my face, I looked again, smiling at myself. It felt good to be me, to be alive. I was okay, and even though I missed my old life, I was starting a new one.

"Is anybody home?"

"Shane, you almost made me pee my pants!"

"Come here, pretty girl. Kiss me hello," he said, pulling me close.

"I haven't brushed my teeth," I replied, pushing away.

"Hurry up, brush those teeth so I can kiss you."

"How many days now?" I asked through a mouth full of toothpaste.

"Seventeen. Can you believe I'm about to graduate!" He stated, waiting for me to rinse my mouth before pulling me into his arms for a kiss.

Slipping out of his arms, I opened the closet door, searching for work clothes. Throwing them on the bed, I rushed back into his arms, kissing him again, saying, "I wish I were going to school today."

"I wish neither of us were going."

"I miss it sometimes."

His hands went under the back of my t-shirt as he pulled me closer. "I'm going to miss you today."

"I miss you every day," I said, staring into his green eyes.

"One of these days, I'm going to marry you."

"What did you just say?"

"You just wait and see, Kessum Christy Howards. One day, I'm going to make you a Williams," he said, stepping back and staring at me with a grin.

"Kessum Williams, it does have a certain church bell ring to it," I replied, hardly believing those words just came out of my mouth.

"It really does. See you tonight, beautiful."

We shared one last embrace, held for a few seconds longer than usual, and I said, "See you tonight, handsome."

For the next couple of weeks, Shane talked about graduating almost nonstop. It was like nothing else crossed his mind. It made me happy for him, but sad for me at the same time. I did my best to hide my true feelings. I didn't want to ruin his big day just because I wouldn't receive my diploma.

After graduation, the days flew by in a blur of work. On the weekends, Shane and Cooley always had something planned for us to do. A group of about twenty of us spent most of our Saturdays either on Big Lake or at Biloxi Beach. Shane's dad didn't mind if we gathered at the cabin, but his mom always preferred we go to the beach. Annie didn't like all of us being at the cabin because of what happened the night I was arrested.

Shane's parents reserved every Monday night for their once-a-week family dinner. With four restaurants and church on Sunday, Monday was the best time to get together. Sometimes, we met at one of their restaurants, but more often, we had dinner at their home, which everybody called the big house. Sometimes, Annie cooked; other times, she had something delivered from one of their restaurants.

We met at the big house for dinner the last Monday before Shane left for college. There was something different about tonight, evident in how we spoke and looked at each other. It felt bittersweet, full of thankfulness and a little regret.

"These summer days passed by so quickly. I can't believe you'll be leaving in a few more days," Annie said.

Shane's little brother, Tyler, sighed, dropping his phone, asking, "What's the big deal? He's only going to Hattiesburg."

"Annie don't get so emotional. He'll only be an hour away. You knew this day was coming since Shane was born," Arthur spoke softly, rubbing her back.

Shane moved closer to Annie, looking at her. He turned back to look at me with tears in his eyes. I didn't know what to do. I wasn't sure whether I should speak or remain silent.

"I'll be back to see you, Mom. I've already promised Kessum I'd try to come home every weekend."

"He did promise, and I was hoping to go to Hattiesburg with you sometime. Since I don't have a car or a license, I don't know how else I would get there."

"We need to fix that, Kessum," Arthur said, walking to put a hand on each of our shoulders. "Next week, I'll take you to get your permit."

"That would be awesome. Thank you so much," I said.

Annie came around the table and stood beside Arthur. We all stood silently, except for Tyler, who started playing a game on his phone. It was as if we all wanted to capture this time, to remember it forever. We knew these Monday night meals, our special time together, were coming to an end for now. His mother stared at us as though trying to remember every detail. It felt oddly strange, and then suddenly, I felt so much love for Annie.

"One day," Annie whispered, "Kessum will be part of our family."

"Yes, I think she will," Arthur said.

Annie smiled, reaching out to touch Shane's cheek. "Yes, I most definitely think so. You two make a beautiful couple, and you will have gorgeous babies. I, for one, cannot wait."

"Okay, Mom, slow down," Shane said, winking.

"Don't think I brought up the subject of marriage first. Shane already told us he wants to marry you, Kessum," Annie said, looking at Shane.

"No, ma'am, I wouldn't think… I mean, he can marry who he wants or who you want. That's totally up to him, you, and his dad. I'm sorry, I'm babbling. I don't know what I'm saying."

Shane put his arms around me and pulled me toward him, saying, "I should have told you, Kessum, but I wanted to wait for the right moment."

The food was getting cold, so we resumed small talk as usual. I mainly listened because an inner dialogue in my head made it hard to pay attention. One thought running through my mind made me anxious, and the next made me happy. Somehow, I managed to calm myself and join the conversation about the future.

There was a nervous tension because we all knew the time we had left together was running out. It was getting late, and Shane would leave for college in the morning. We all began to make promises. Then we started to make plans for upcoming visits. Those plans gave us something to look forward to in the next few months.

The next four years of Shane's life had been mapped out long before we knew each other. He would attend the University of Southern Mississippi and get a degree in business. After college, he would return to Biloxi to live in a house his parents would give him as a graduation gift. Then, he would take over one of the four restaurants Arthur and Annie owned. Between now and then, we would talk on the phone every day, see each other every weekend, and stay together, no matter what! It was settled.

The biggest issue with the promises and plans we'd made before Shane left for college was the distance between us. Seeing each other every weekend turned into every other weekend, and daily phone calls became three or four calls a week. Slowly, we drifted apart as college consumed his life and helping run one of his dad's restaurants consumed mine. Every promise we made to each other was made with the best intentions. Still, life with its endless demands had a way of changing plans.

In the mad rush of day-to-day life, it felt like I blinked and Christmas decorations were going up everywhere. Shane was home again, and we picked up right where we left off, as if no time had passed. Arthur gave me extra time off work so Shane and I could be together. Now, it was time to relax and have fun. For him, that meant having friends over or going out to a party every night.

Our days flew by in a blur of shopping, parties, and Christmas at the big house. On the last night of the year, when we kissed at midnight during the New Year's party, I felt exhausted. Shane, however, felt the exact opposite. Exhilarated by the crowd and music, he couldn't stay in his seat. He kept going back to the dance floor. I watched him raise his fist, pumping it to the beat. For some reason, a lot of the guys, including his dad, joined him.

"Kessum, what are you doing sitting over here alone? Shouldn't you be out on the dancefloor?" Annie asked, sitting down a little too close.

"Are you okay, Annie?"

"Yes, just too much of this stuff," she said, raising a glass of champagne.

From the edge of the dance floor, Shane looked over at us and raised his glass. Annie raised her glass, smiling, giving him a wink. His head nodded to the beat of the dance song Titanium, and he motioned for us to join him.

Annie wrapped her arm around my shoulder and gently squeezed. Then she took my hand and leaned toward my ear. "Looks like my son needs a dance partner."

My young but exhausted body didn't want to budge from what little relief it found on this red velvet couch. Shane's smile picked me up and made my feet move toward the love of my life one step at a time. He wrapped his arm around my waist and pulled me against his body. We rocked back and forth to the music as he sang the words with our friends.

The music changed, our bodies swayed, eyes met, and my heart sank. His eyes looked worried, which was something I rarely saw. For weeks, I wondered what was happening in Hattiesburg. Was he being faithful? Was he even thinking about me or our promises to each other? Now, in his embrace, I could see he was troubled.

Shane leaned forward, closing his eyes, and pressed his lips against mine. We moved and kissed like no one except us was on the dance floor. There, in the middle of it all, was a single tear. It fell from his cheek onto mine.

"Break it up, you two! Or I'm going to call the police and have you arrested," Cooley yelled, pulling us apart just to wrap us in his arms.

"What are you doing here, dude? I thought you were offshore."

"I got fired! I got in a fight with an old redneck! This guy was something else! One minute, everything was fine, then my hand turned into a fist that went to meet his ugly face. Man, I don't know what I was thinking, but now I'm out of a job."

Shane slapped him on the back, saying, "Bummer, dude. I figured you'd be running that rig in no time."

Cooley took my hand, pulling me away from Shane. "Let's go sit down and talk. You look like you need a break."

As we walked, I reached back for Shane's hand, and we followed Cooley to a table at the back of the room. We sat on a black leather couch, then Cooley said, "Maybe we can catch up before everybody knows I'm here."

"Mr. Popular," Shane joked.

"Well, you know! The ladies love me, little old ladies wish they could be my granny, and all the puppies want to follow me home. What can I say? When you got it, you got it."

"Seems like I remember your grandpa saying the same thing when we were growing up," Shane laughed, doing their unique handshake.

"I know Kessum is doing good. I see her at work when I come home. How's college life?" Cooley asked.

"It's all a blur, man. Books, professors, libraries, exams, and parties. I don't suggest it unless you don't like sleeping and enjoy being stressed out."

"Guess I made the right decision, skipping college. You did the right thing, too. When you finish, you'll be set for life. I don't know what I'm going to end up doing. I might have to go work at the restaurant with Kessum," Cooley laughed, patting my knee.

"I'd love that; we'd have so much fun!"

Shane scooted closer, put his arm around my shoulder, and pulled me towards him. He looked at me without a smile, then back at Cooley. "I don't think she will work there much longer."

"Woe, are you two planning on tying the knot soon? Did something happen I don't know about?"

"No, we're not having a shotgun wedding, but if we get married sooner, what's it to you?"

With Shane's words reverberating through my mind, I was stunned into silence. He never mentioned anything else to me about getting married. It was weird, and I'd never heard him speak to Cooley like that before.

"Kessum, are you okay? Can you hear me?" Shane asked, lifting my chin toward his face.

"Yes, I hear you."

"She is freaking out, dude," Cooley said.

"I'm just a little shook. When were you going to tell me?"

"Dang, dude. What a way to spring it on your girl. Should've thought about it before you opened your mouth," Cooley said, staring at Shane.

"It's New Year's. I thought tonight might be the perfect timing. We could run away and elope."

Cooley slammed his hand on the table, saying, "Well, I guess it might be perfect timing for me to get out of here. Are you two staying out at the cabin tonight?"

"No, not tonight," Shane said, standing up. He reached for my hand, and I stood up before he replied, "We're here with Mom and Dad."

"Then I guess you'll be staying at the mansion," Cooley replied in a fake British accent. "Lifestyles of the children of the rich and somewhat famous."

"Whatever you say, Cooley. Don't forget, we grew up in the same neighborhood, and your daddy's house is bigger than my dad's."

"True, but you got the cool dad, and I got the cruel dad. He expects me to be a self-made multi-millionaire by twenty-five."

"Sometimes life just isn't fair," Shane said, walking toward the dance floor, pulling me with him.

Cooley rushed up to grab my other hand, squeezing it twice before letting go. He smiled, walked in the other direction, only looking back at me once. I watched as he left, thinking about how close he and Shane were just a few months ago. They were practically inseparable for years. Now, in no time at all, life had led them down different paths. They were changing, and even though I believed they would always be friends, it was different. The difference made me feel strangely sad. If it had happened to them in such a short time, it could happen to anyone, no matter how close the relationship.

A few days later, when Shane was packed and ready to head back to USM, neither of us was ready to be apart again. We didn't know how we would make it through the next few months without each other. The one thing we knew for certain was that if we wanted to keep our relationship strong, we needed to spend more time together. Barely seeing each other wasn't working.

Love had us making promises we knew we couldn't keep. We said we'd see each other every weekend, no matter what it took. We made plans to talk on the phone every day. Then we promised to send messages to each other, morning, noon, and night. Those promises gave us a small measure of security, allowing our relationship to survive another separation. Even with the odds stacked against us, I still believed love would be the guiding force to make everything work out.

In the first few weeks, we managed to keep our promises. As the days and weeks passed, those promises became harder and harder to keep. Then the distance between us began to feel farther and farther as we slowly drifted apart.

Loneliness crept in on me like an autumn wind bringing a chill. It felt like there wasn't anything I could do to warm up. Each day without Shane felt like a week, and each week like a month.

His mother, Annie, noticed how sad I'd been since Shane left and began spending more time with me. At first, it was a welcome distraction from feeling alone. Then the real reason for her sudden interest in my life was revealed.

Annie wanted to prepare me just in case I became a part of their family. She started by teaching me how to live the right way. She explained that the Bible teaches that marriage comes first, before becoming intimate or living together. It was expected that married couples would stay together and be faithful to one another for their entire lives.

When she insisted I go to church with her on Sundays, I wasn't sure what to do. A part of me wanted to go, but another part didn't want to be controlled by anyone. To keep the peace, I told her I would go. Annie decided I couldn't work on Sunday and made sure I wasn't on the schedule. It was one of my best days for making tips. I knew I needed to stand up for myself and say something, but I didn't. Nothing I could say would persuade her to see my perspective. She had no idea what it was like to need money. Annie Williams had been born into wealth. She didn't know anything else and believed there was only one way to do things: the right way. In her mind, the right way was her way. There was no in-between, and she expected me to do everything right if I wanted to be a part of their family someday.

With little hesitation, I went to church with Annie and joined the groups she attended. Ultimately, the experience left me feeling alone in another group of people. In fact, the only time I didn't feel alone in church was when we sang. Something extraordinary happened in the sanctuary when we were singing. The music was the one thing that brought me back every Sunday.

After a couple of months, I began to feel differently about church. It was the first time in my life that anyone taught me about God. It felt good, and they made me feel better about the future. The intense feeling of being alone, without Shane, began to subside. Being in the church gave me hope about how my life could be like one day.

Time flew by quickly as I stayed busy with work and church. Then, with the end of another semester of college, Shane came home to Biloxi. Within a few days, it almost felt like he never left. We were together and looking forward to another summer of sunshine and fun. We fell into our usual routine of basking in the sun by Big Lake or boating on the Gulf. Our weekends were filled with friends, new and old, parties, and dancing under the stars. We went to church together on his first Sunday home, which made me happy. I'd never understood why we never missed a Monday night meal with Shane's family but had never been to church together.

Shane kept us busy day after day, but I didn't mind. He was back in my arms, and nothing else mattered. We didn't talk about how lonely I'd been. We didn't talk about how busy he'd been with college. We definitely didn't talk about how we broke our promises to stay in touch this semester. It was behind us.

When he was in Biloxi, Shane's parents expected him to stay at their house, while I stayed at the cabin. This was for appearances' sake and because of Annie's beliefs about what is right and wrong. It bothered me sometimes because I was never invited to stay at the big house, even though there were several guest rooms. However, some of those nights, I would ask a friend to come and stay with me so I wouldn't be alone.

May in Mississippi can be unpredictable when it comes to the weather. One day, it could feel like summer. The next day, it would remind you that it's still springtime. Tomorrow's forecast predicted one of those summer-like days, so I invited Trina to stay the night with me. The next morning we decided to lay out and get some sun. We took our chairs down to the lakeshore and turned on music.

"What time is it, Trina?"

She stretched her arms over her head as she yawned loudly, then replied, "It's time to flip over. We don't want to be two different colors."

"No, we want to look sun-kissed, not sunbaked."

"I don't even know why you care, Kessum. I wouldn't even go to their stupid garden party if it were me."

"But you are going. With me, right?"

Trina sighed loudly, adjusted her sunglasses, then said, "I guess so, but I don't have to be happy about it."

"It's going to be fun. Plus, there'll be cute guys."

"You mean rich, stuck-up boys! I'll pass, thank you very much."

"You like Shane, and Cooley, and what's that guy's name... the one with red hair. Remember, you kissed him at that dance."

Trina sat up, putting her sunglasses on her head, without saying a word. Then she lay back down on the chair, turning to face me. "His name is Harry, like the prince. I don't understand why you never remember his name."

"I don't know. Probably because he doesn't look like Harry, the prince."

"I kissed him once in eighth grade. It's not like we dated. I know you're just trying to help, but going to Arthur and Annie's house for a Fancy Nancy party isn't my idea of fun."

A boat sped past us, and waves began to crash upon the shore. I thought about what Trina just said as I contemplated what to say next. I wanted her to come to the party because I didn't want to go alone. Shane had a way of staying with me for the first few minutes, then wandering off, talking to people I don't know. Then I realized that if I didn't want to go, I shouldn't try to convince her to go with me.

"It's okay, Trina. You don't have to come."

She grabbed my arm, sat up slightly, and said, "No, I'm coming. I've already bought a dress. We'll eat fancy food, sip champagne, and act like we own the place."

"Yay! I'm so happy you're going. We should probably go in soon to get ready."

"Just a few more minutes in the sun, okay?"

"Sounds good to me," I answered, turning up the music.

We laid in the sun until my stomach began to growl. Trina was hungry, too, so we went inside and made something to eat. She got in the shower first while I cleaned the kitchen. After I showered, we turned on music, put on our makeup, and laughed like we were still in high school when we were getting ready to go out.

After we had done our hair and makeup, I put on the dress Annie bought. When I stepped out of the bathroom, Trina started laughing and shook her head from side to side. She said I looked like a 40-year-old realtor from Palm Beach, Florida.

Trina searched through my closet while complaining about Annie's choice of dresses. She found three other dresses and put them on the bed. After trying on all three, we decided on a little black dress. We both put on perfume, looking at ourselves one last time in the mirror before we hurried out the door.

We were running late, but getting there didn't take long. There were more people at the big house than I expected. Men, women, and children filled every bit of space from the driveway all the way into the house.

Shane was waiting for us at the entryway and took me by the hand, kissing my cheek. He led me through the crowded house without stopping to speak to anyone and out the back door. He guided me through the large crowd, past many beautifully decorated tables, to a table in the center. I sat down and looked around, expecting to see Trina, but she was nowhere to be seen.

Minutes later, Annie sat beside me, asking, "Where's the dress I bought you?"

"Trina said it didn't look good, so I wore this instead."

"This is not a nightclub, young lady."

The tone in her voice was one I'd never heard before. When she leaned away from me, she had a big smile, but hearing the disappointment in her voice stole mine.

People walked by, greeting me with compliments and hugs. It wasn't easy, but I did my best to appear happy. I searched the crowd for Trina. She was supposed to be here, sitting beside me in that empty chair, but she wasn't anywhere in sight. Every tall, slender blonde caught my eye, but none was my best friend.

Shane finally came back and sat in the empty chair beside me, moving it closer to me. He kissed my cheek, took my hand, pulling it toward his chest. His green eyes pierced through the chaos and saw what I was trying to hide.

"Something's wrong."

"No, I'm okay, Shane."

He leaned over, pushed my hair back, and whispered, "Kessum, I know you better than you think. What happened?"

"Your Mom was very rude about my dress."

"You're not wearing the one she gave you."

"I didn't like it."

Shane leaned back and said, "Don't be upset with me. I like this dress. It looks good on you."

A tall guy with red hair grabbed my attention. Even though it had been a while since I'd seen Harry, there was no denying it was him. Towering over most people was one thing that made him memorable, but the shoulder-length red hair made him stand out in a crowd. I stood up to see if he had anyone with him. The moment Harry saw me, he pointed a finger toward our table. Trina looked around him, giving me a thumbs up.

Shane tugged my hand, asking, "Where will they sit?"

"I don't know."

Shane asked a couple to our left if they would move to another table so Trina and Harry could sit near us. After exchanging hellos and introductions, they sat down. Arthur interrupted when I started telling Trina how upset Shane's Mom was.

"Is this thing on? Can you hear me out there? All right, all right, I see your hands waving and a couple of nods. I just wanted to say thank you for coming out and spending this special evening with us. I hope everyone is having a good time and getting plenty to eat and drink. My wife, Annie, and I want everybody to know we love our son, Shane. We are so proud of him and can't wait for him to finish college and move back home."

Shane stood up, hugging his dad, and then hugged his mom. It felt like every eye in the place was staring at us. I sat there suddenly wishing I'd escaped to the bathroom. Annie turned toward me and reached out for my hand. With my hand in hers, she helped me up, then stepped back. Shane turned to face me, and his dad held out the microphone.

"Kessum, I love you with all my heart."

Shane took my hand and got down on one knee. Then, multiple cameras and cell phones focused on us as he continued, "Kessum Christy Howards, please make me the most blessed man in the world! Will you marry me?"

Arthur handed the microphone to Annie, who smiled and posed perfectly for pictures. Looking at Shane, I couldn't say no, but then a thought crossed my mind. I wondered if any of this was his idea. His eyes looked worried as I hesitated to answer. The whole place was silent.

I blurted out, "Yes! Yes, I will marry you."

"Woo! I was getting nervous." He reached into his pocket and pulled out a jewelry box. He opened it, saying, "I hope you like it. It was my grandmother's ring."

My eyes studied every curve, sharp edge, and stone encased in yellow gold. It wasn't a classic large stone set in a simple band. The center diamond looked like a carat or more, surrounded by smaller diamonds. It looked old-fashioned and gaudy, something I would never pick out, but I smiled.

Shane took the ring from the tiny black box and stood up. Annie was still holding the microphone. He took my hand, put the ring on my finger, and stared into my eyes. It felt like the whole room was watching. I thought the chair was behind me, but when I stepped back, somebody was there.

"Are you okay?" Trina asked.

"I need to sit down," I said, looking over my shoulder for a chair.

"Shane's Mom is waiting for your answer," Trina said, moving closer, holding my arm up so everyone standing nearby could see the ring.

As my heart fluttered, I asked, "What was the question?"

"Do you like the ring?" Annie asked. "It was my mother's ring, Shane's grandmother."

"Yes, it's different, it's beautiful."

The look on my future mother-in-law's face spoke volumes. She wasn't happy. Unfortunately, I was not doing a good job of hiding my emotions. Disappointed, angry, and heartbroken were just the beginning of what I felt. Without saying a word, Annie knew why I was upset. My parents were not here, and there was no excuse she could give me to make it okay.

Annie turned away from me, entertaining the crowd with ohs and ahs over the ring. Arthur knew I was upset but acted like nothing was wrong, calling for a round of champagne. Apparently appearance was more important than my feelings, which was a great revelation to me. The inexcusable thing was my parents weren't invited to my engagement party. The fact that they acted like it didn't matter was almost unforgivable.

The only thing I could do for Shane's sake was put on a brave face and be kind to our guests. The several hours I had to fake being happy while crying on the inside took every bit of energy I had within me. When the party finally ended, I realized I needed to wait until the morning to see my parents.

Even though I barely slept and rehearsed what I would say, I knew there was no way of knowing what might happen. I couldn't predict how Mom and Dad would react, but I hoped they would understand. With one last prayer, I knocked on the front door.

Before seeing their faces, I figured they knew nothing about my engagement. Now I knew they did. We sat down, and I didn't even get a chance to speak. When I opened my mouth, Dad put his hand out.

"Kessum, we know you're engaged to that… boy. What we can't understand is why you didn't include us! You may think we're the worst parents in the world, but we did nothing to deserve not being invited to our only daughter's engagement party."

"I didn't…."

"Stop! I don't want to hear your excuses. Your mom and I spent the best years of our lives working hard to give you a good life. What did we get in return? You started hanging out with the wrong people, dropped out of school, and left home. Now you're engaged to an alcoholic's son. How do you think that's going to turn out for you?"

Mom scooted up to the edge of her seat, pulling her shoulders back. She turned back to look at Dad, then turned to face me, saying, "That's enough, Richard. You haven't even let Kessum speak."

"Then speak up, Kessum. I can't wait to hear your excuses."

Tears filled my eyes, and I fought hard not to let them fall. I cleared my throat before saying, "This has been harder on me than you know. I was devastated when I found out you weren't there last night. I don't know why Annie and Arthur didn't invite you. When I asked, I didn't get an answer. I wanted to come over last night, but it was too late."

Mom scooted back and reached for Dad's hand. She looked at me with neither a smile nor a frown. In that moment, I only wanted everything to be okay between us.

Dad cleared his throat, asking, "Are you going to marry him?"

"Yes, I love Shane."

Mom stood up and began pacing before saying, "You're too young to get married, Kessum. Give yourself time to grow up and mature. Figure out what you want to do with your life and who you are before Shane's family tells you who you should be."

"We haven't picked a date, Mom, but I'll take as much time as possible."

We talked for a long time about more than the engagement. During our conversation, a bridge was built between my parents and me. It shifted our relationship, and for the first time, I realized how much they had my back. My dad could be a little hard on me, but deep down, he had my best interests at heart.

It was that very day when I could finally see how many times I'd mistaken their concern for selfishness. I always wanted what I wanted. Sometimes, I was like a runaway train, heading directly toward what I desired, regardless of the consequences. After our heart-to-heart, I realized my parents were the only voices of reason in many seasons of my life.

CHAPTER FOUR

Annie insisted we set the date within a year of engagement. It was how they did it in her family and how it would be for her son. As I promised Mom, I pushed the date as far out as possible. It was a small win, but somehow, I convinced my future mother-in-law that we needed more time.

The wedding had to be at the best venue in Biloxi, hire the best caterer, and serve the most expensive food. Then, Annie took me to meet the most celebrated baker in town. They barely spoke to me but talked about a humongous four-tier cake. It was more than I wanted, but when she handed me the updated guest list, I realized things were getting out of control. My future mother-in-law and I needed a little heart-to-heart chat, so I arranged a meeting.

"Kessum, thank you for inviting me to lunch. Now that you're going to be my daughter-in-law, we'll get to do this a lot."

The waiter set two huge bowls of salad in front of us. Annie picked up the pepper, shaking it vigorously over her bowl. She held it out, and I took it, sprinkling a little, then added, "I can't wait to be part of your family."

"It's going to be fun. I'm sorry your mom was upset about the engagement party. I shouldn't have to explain, but now you know I wanted it to be a surprise. If your mom and dad were there, you would have known something was up. Have you seen some of the videos? The look on your face! Priceless," she said, reaching over to touch my arm.

"I get it, Annie, but it still hurt my parents. My mom and dad should have been invited."

"Well, of course, they should have been there. I know that…"

"Okay, and they have to be invited to their only daughter's wedding."

Annie tilted her head, leaned back, and laughed before adding, "Of course they're invited. Certainly, you wouldn't think I'd exclude them from the guest list?"

Trying to hide my emotions, I cleared my throat before saying, "Well, that's a deep subject; maybe it's better for another place and time. The reason I asked to meet today is the wedding."

Annie took a small bite of salad but chewed as if it were a huge forkful. Her eyes smiled, but something was off. She looked at me, took her napkin, wiped both corners of her mouth, then took a small sip of sweet tea, asking, "What about the wedding?"

"Annie, it's all the wedding plans. My parents can't afford even half of what you're…"

"Kessum, don't worry about anything. I have a plan- well, maybe more like a proposal. I intended to talk to both of you, but I know Shane will be happy with our decision."

"It's just that we need to scale everything back. Like way back. Umm, my parents didn't save much for…"

"Listen, you don't have to explain. I've got everything under control." Annie smiled widely, took another bite of salad, and chewed as though she were counting.

The fork felt heavy in my hand as I lifted it. My mind was racing, but I was doing what I could to hide it. What did she mean by saying she had it under control? I cleared my throat before saying, "I know I don't have to explain. You know our circumstances. My parents can afford a wedding, but not as expensive as you're planning."

"Look, I want to take this burden off your parents. They can buy the wedding dress, and Arthur and I will pay for the rest. You'll have your dream wedding, whatever you want, and we'll send you on a fantastic honeymoon. Once Shane graduates from college, we will buy a nice home for you to raise a family. On top of that, we'll sign over the deed to one of our restaurants for you and Shane. I only have one stipulation."

"What is it?"

"I want you to stay in Biloxi until the wedding. It wouldn't look good for you to be engaged and stay in Hattiesburg together. That would also give Shane the time and space to focus on college. Plus, it will give you and me more time to get to know one another."

"I don't know, Annie. Shane just asked me if I would move. I didn't know he had said anything to you."

"He did, and Arthur and I already discussed it. We don't think it's a wise decision for either of you."

"I need to talk to Shane…"

"We already talked to him and he agreed with us. We decided that if it's okay with you and you promise to stay here, you won't need to work. We will open an account for you to have more than enough money. There's so much to be done before the wedding; honestly, you don't have time to work at the restaurant."

"I know the wedding will be beautiful, but I'm not sure about quitting my job. I've been saving money for things we'll need after we're married."

"Well, you can use that money on yourself, honey. We will make sure the house is furnished and everything is taken care of until Shane is financially secure."

"That's so generous of you, Annie. My parents could never do anything like that for me."

"We started planning for our boys' futures before they were born. It's the right thing to do."

"I hope Shane and I can do that for our children."

"You will, I know Shane will make sure of that. Kessum, I also think it's important for you to stay here so you can continue going to the First Baptist Church of Biloxi. Shane has gone there his entire life, and when you have his children, he will want them to go there."

"Shane and I have only been to church together a few times."

"He was there almost every week, not long before he met you. Look, I'm not saying you're the reason he isn't in church, don't get upset, but I know my son. He will want his wife and children to attend his church. He's a Christian, regardless of the phase he's going through in life. Chapter 22 of Proverbs says, 'Train up a child in the way he should go; and when he is old he will not depart from it.'"

"I believe in God."

"Honey, not everyone who believes in God is a Christian. Remember, 'Many are called, but few are chosen.' Did your parents take you to church when you were little?"

My appetite was suddenly gone. I set my fork down, wiped both sides of my mouth, and placed my napkin across the bowl. Annie stared at me, then took another bite. As she swallowed, I took another sip of water.

"Yes, my parents took me to church when I was young. We didn't stop going until my grandmother died when I was about eight years old. After that, I'd still go with my Aunt May sometimes."

Annie looked down at her salad bowl. She'd barely eaten. She wiped her mouth, saying, "Just let me know. It'll be an adjustment, not working, but it'd be better to start planning your wedding sooner rather than later. We want everything to be perfect."

"I'll let you know."

"Good, I think it's what's best for both of you. Arthur and I would be thrilled to throw you the wedding of the year. Maybe even the wedding of the decade! One that no one in Biloxi, Mississippi will forget anytime soon."

Refusal was useless when it was in opposition to Annie Williams' plans. I wasn't exactly packing my bags to leave for Hattiesburg, but I felt the decision should have been mine and Shane's, along with the decision of whether I should continue working or not. However, in his family, it was her way or the highway. Annie was the unofficial boss of the Williams' family, and I was only a soon-to-be non-blood relative.

It shocked me that Shane didn't hesitate or argue her demands. My future husband approved of everything his mother wanted. In less than two weeks, our secret plans of living together dissipated like vapor, and I was no longer employed. It was easy to get over not moving to Hattiesburg, but not going to work hit me hard. The only consolation for doing what Annie wanted was that my parents were off the hook for a quarter of a million-dollar wedding.

Those first few weeks without Shane flew by in a blur of work and planning for our wedding. After I stopped working, I did my best to stay busy. At nighttime, my mind always wandered back into memories. The way he held me until I fell asleep. His lips against my lips, with the sun shining on us, warming our skin. The way he looked at me when we were in a crowd, like we had a secret he'd never tell.

Those memories kept me tossing and turning some nights until I couldn't take it anymore. I'd turn on the light, get out of bed, and do whatever it took to get my mind off Shane. Other times, I'd put his picture on the pillow beside me and cry myself to sleep.

The next day, he'd call to ask how I was doing. Many times, I had to choke back tears, but I would always tell him I was okay. Between college and our future, he had so much on his mind, and I didn't want to burden him with anything else.

The only problem with hiding my feelings from him was that our phone conversations had become repetitive and almost meaningless. He didn't know how much I was struggling without him here. I went out with our friends, but it felt like I was single because I was the only one without a date. And nearly everything we did made me think of my memories with Shane, which only made me miss him even more.

Our core group of friends was growing up quickly, becoming young adults. Many of them had moved away or were in college. Shane and I had become best friends after becoming engaged, which only made our long-distance relationship harder. It felt like I was stuck in Biloxi, and not doing anything to further my education only made it worse.

Some days, I could rationalize that it would be very soon before I saw Shane again. Other days, my heart ached, and nothing could console it. On those days, the usual distractions failed to get him off my mind. My arms longed to hold him, and my lips wanted to be kissed by him.

When I couldn't take one more day of waiting, one more day of wishing, and wanting, I would go to the lake or the beach. I sat alone near the water. I would think about what we had shared and dream about the future. It wouldn't always be this way. We wouldn't live an hour away from each other's doorstep forever.

Still, through it all, Shane found ways to stay in touch. He came home to Biloxi as often as possible and called me nearly every day. When he was here. Sometimes we stayed at the cabin alone, not even telling anyone he was home. Other times we stayed out on the boat with friends or went to parties. A lot of times, he didn't want to do anything except hang out at his parents' house, which was alright with me. All that mattered was being together.

Truth be told, our long-distance relationship was taking its toll on both Shane and me. We did our best to see each other, and we did even better at hiding what each of us was going through. We could never make enough phone calls or send enough text messages to replace being in each other's arms. Nothing could replace holding hands or the sensation of his lips kissing mine.

Ironically, the one thing that helped me keep it together was Wednesday night Bible study. Annie insisted I go with her, and at first I resisted, but now I was thankful. Almost every Wednesday, she would pick me up for an early dinner at 4:00, and then we would attend church.

The group was led by a lady named Linda, and I started looking forward to seeing her every week. She had just celebrated her 37th birthday but looked like she could pass for twenty-seven.

She and her husband, Jordan, had been married 12 years and had two sons: Brett, 11, and Seth, 9.

Despite the age gap, we had a few things in common. Linda was raised in a strict household. Her dad was overprotective and sheltered his children from the bad things happening in the world in every way possible. She was not raised in church, but her family believed in God, just like me.

On the other hand, Jordan started attending First Baptist of Biloxi as a baby. His family had been going there for generations, just like Shane. Linda felt obligated to join the church after they married, so she did. She also told me that it just made sense. As a third-grade teacher, many of her students and their families attended First Baptist.

It was helpful to have someone unbiased to talk to about life. My friends were too busy living life in pursuit of their goals to spend much time with me. Mom had nothing but negative opinions about the Williams family. This left me fighting a mental war, trying to decide what was right and what was wrong—that is, until I became friends with Linda.

Linda called one Thursday morning to ask if I could meet her for lunch. She had a doctor's appointment in Gulfport at noon. We rarely saw each other except on Wednesday nights, so I said yes, even on short notice.

After we ate Cajun red beans and rice at a downtown café, we decided to walk around looking at the shops. We could have spent hours exploring all the beautiful things for sale. However, there was a florist nearby that Linda wanted to go to before getting dessert.

The bell on the front door rang, alerting a sweet older lady who nodded at us and smiled. The aroma smelled like walking into a field of flowers on a warm spring day. The older lady talked with another customer, so Linda and I walked toward the fresh-cut flowers.

"Which one do you like best, white roses or daisies?"

"They're both beautiful. Which one do you prefer?" Linda asked.

She walked around me, reaching out to pick up a yellow rose. Then she reached for a white daisy and held it together. When she picked up a few extra yellow roses, I watched.

"I like them both, but Annie already picked lavender and white for the wedding colors."

"What do you think of these?"

"Those are beautiful. I love yellow roses."

"What about white roses?"

"That's what Annie said."

Linda went to the white roses, picking up about a half dozen. She added them to the yellow one and the daisies, asking, "Do we have a winner, or do you want to look at the pink ones?"

"The pink ones caught my eye, but I don't think Annie will like them. What do you think?"

"I think it's your choice. You can't go wrong with roses, no matter what color they are."

"It's too late to change the color scheme, but I really like the yellow, it's my favorite," I replied, staring at the bouquet.

"I love yellow roses, too. Are you ready for dessert?"

"Absolutely. Where do you want to go?"

Linda put the flowers back in a bucket of water, saying, "I don't know, but I want ice cream."

"Oh, that sounds good. Maybe a scoop of vanilla or chocolate, maybe both."

"Now you sound like me." Linda laughed softly, holding the door. As we walked down the street, Linda asked, "Have you read the Bible, Kessum?"

"Not really, I mean, I don't own one, except for my childhood Bible, which is at my parents' house."

"What are your beliefs about God?"

"My mom and dad taught me that God is in heaven and watches over us. We have angels that protect us from death if it's not our time. Oh, and they told me about Jesus, like the Easter story. He died, then in three days He left the tomb, and He is risen."

"Have you learned more about the Bible in our life group?"

I hesitated before answering, "A little, but honestly, it's a bit overwhelming. I mean, I'm sitting in a room full of people who have been in church their whole lives."

"I've never even thought about it, but you're right. If it's okay with you, I'd like to spend a little more time together. I could call Jordan to pick up the boys. If you have time, we can go to the park."

"I could do that, but I don't want to keep…"

"You're not keeping me from anything. Trust me, I need a break, but I don't want to keep you from anything." Linda looked at her watch, smiled, and then turned to look down the street before looking back at me.

"There's nothing I have to do except go home and be alone in that big old cabin. Let's go. Maybe there will be an ice cream truck."

"Sounds like a plan. I'll meet you there," Linda replied, waiting for a car to pass before crossing the street.

It was about a two-mile drive to the park. So many questions ran through my mind as I drove. Why did Linda want to go to the park? Why did she want to spend more time together? Did she want to talk about God?

Before I parked the car, I decided that if she brought up God, I'd change the subject. When anyone had ever tried to explain what He's like, it never helped. Honestly, in my mind, the only picture I had of Him was an old white-haired man needing a haircut. He watched over the people He created from His throne in heaven. He knew they suffered but did little to change anything. Yes, people claimed that God performed miracles, but I had never seen one personally. Still, the hatred and evil in this world convinced me that if there is a God, He only cares about His people, the chosen.

We walked to the lake and found a bench to sit on. It was early in the afternoon, a little cool, but the sun warmed us up. We only saw three or four people walking on the track. A few kids played on the playground as a couple of moms watched. No ice cream truck was in sight, but I hoped one would come by soon.

"Tell me what you know about Jesus."

The question hung uncomfortably in the air. Linda waited, looking out toward the water. I shifted uncomfortably, matching her gaze. My mind scrambled, trying to think of a way to avoid the subject. We both watched two black crows land on the ground not too far away, then she crossed her legs.

"He was a man who prayed for people, and they were healed. They killed Him, and Christians believe He came back to life, and now He's in heaven. It's a crazy story if you think about it.

Oh, and people believe He's coming back, but Jesus was killed a long time ago."

Linda shifted slightly toward me, uncrossed her legs, and smiled before saying, "For me, the stories in the Bible are glimpses into who Jesus is and what He did during His ministry. He's our savior, an example of how to live, but more than anything, Jesus is my friend. Not like the kind of friends you have here on Earth. Think of the best person you have ever known or can imagine. He's a hundred times more loyal and trustworthy than anyone on Earth because He will never betray you. He will never abandon you."

"Sounds like someone I'd like to know."

"You can know Him, Kessum. He has a plan and a purpose for your life. Have you ever given Jesus your heart?"

"Umm, there was this one time when I was about five or six. I went to church with my Aunt May. Oh my goodness, I miss my Aunt May, my mom's sister. You remind me of her in a way, except she had darker brown hair and was about a foot shorter than you. Anyway, she was the one who took me to church and taught me most of what I know about God."

A duck waddled up from the edge of the water. It shook, sending water flying in every direction before it walked up the embankment. A few moments later, it was followed by three more. I watched as Linda gently laughed as the crows flew away.

"A simple prayer is all it takes. I hope you know that heaven is a real place... and so is hell."

It seemed like a strange response, and her voice made me wonder what she was thinking about as she watched the birds. After a few moments of silence, I answered, "I want to believe in heaven, but I'm not so sure about hell."

"Do you know where you would go if you died today?" She asked, turning to face me.

"I'm pretty sure I'd go to heaven."

"That's what most people think. Just imagine, Kessum. You and I could spend eternity in paradise with Jesus. That thought brings me so much joy."

Linda reached into her purse, pulled out a small book, and thumbed through the pages. She looked at me and smiled, saying, "In the third chapter of Romans, we learn that every person has sinned and fallen short of the glory of God. The sixth chapter explains that what we deserve for our sins is death, but thanks to Jesus, we can receive the gift from God, eternal life."

"So, does death mean going to hell?"

"No, it doesn't. Hell is not death. Every person who is alive on Earth will die. Hell is eternal separation from God and a place of torment meant for Satan and the fallen angels."

"I remember that guy who spent 90 minutes in hell or something like that."

She set the book between us, putting her hand on mine. "If you ask me, this is one of the best parts of the Bible: 'For whosoever shall call upon the name of the Lord shall be saved.' That's us, Kessum; we are whosoever."

Her tears rolled down both cheeks as I watched. No one had ever spoken to me about Jesus with such sincerity. It made me feel a strange sensation, right in the middle of my chest.

"It's that easy?"

"Yes, all you have to do is believe in Jesus, call out His name, and give Him your life. He's waiting on you."

"What do I need to do?"

"The first thing is to ask Jesus to forgive you of your sins."

"Linda, I'm not sure how to do it. Do you want me to make a list? What am I supposed to say? Do I talk out loud or in my head?"

Looking around, it seemed like she was counting the people at the park. She scooted closer, asking, "Can I hold your hand?"

"Yes."

"Let's pray. Jesus, reveal Yourself to Kessum and renew her heart right now."

"Wow, I feel tingly all over."

"It's okay; He's just doing what He does. Now, you can repeat what I say or ask Him in your own words."

"Okay, I'm ready."

"Lord, please forgive me for my sins and wash me clean. I give you my life," she said.

"God, please forgive me for my sins; make me clean. I give you my life."

Linda squeezed my hand tighter, saying, "That's good, Kessum. Now, say I believe You died for me, I believe You are the Son of God."

"I believe You died for me, and I believe You are the Son of God."

"Last thing, thank you, Jesus, I've been born again and I'm going to heaven!"

"Thank you, Jesus! I'm born again, and I'm going to heaven."

"Hallelujah! Now, let me pray for you. Jesus, we know that where two or more are gathered together, You are here with us. I ask You to bless this beautiful child of Yours with a long and healthy life. Set her free from all bondage, in Jesus' name. Give her a passion for the things of God and protect her from evil. Thank you for my sister, Kessum. In Jesus' name we pray, believing you hear our prayers, and they are answered right now. Amen!"

Linda let go of my hand, wrapped her arm around my shoulder, and hugged me. She held on as we gently swayed, then let go and turned toward me.

"Could you feel that when you were praying? It felt like electricity or something."

She leaned back, looking up at the sky, and said, "Yes, I most definitely felt it."

"Boy, I feel lighter, and I didn't even realize I was feeling heavy. It's like a weight lifted off my shoulders. That is so crazy."

"It's okay to cry."

"I know, but why are you crying?"

Linda picked up her purse, dug in one side, then the other, and pulled out a small package of tissues. Tear after tear fell from my cheeks onto my shirt. My heart felt like it would burst from emotions. Memories flooded my mind, both good and bad. Linda wiped away her tears as she handed me a tissue. She picked up her little bible, searching the pages.

"Matthew 6:15 says, 'But if you do not forgive others their sins, your Father will not forgive your sins.' We must forgive to be forgiven."

"I've heard that before."

"Is there anyone you haven't forgiven? I mean anybody, not just family or the people you're around. After I was saved and understood this scripture, I sat down and made a list and forgave each one of them."

"You went and talked to them?"

"No, not all of them. I only went to see two people on my list. It's more important to forgive them in your heart and talk to God in prayer, telling Him that you have forgiven them. I cannot stress how important it is. It will bring peace into your life like you've never known."

"I can do it. It's not easy to forgive some of the people who have hurt me, but I'll try."

Linda dug in her purse, pulling out a pen and a notepad. "It's easier than you think," she said, writing and repeating what she had written, "Lord, I forgive -blank- for -blank- and will not hold on to unforgiveness toward them. Thank you, God, that I am your child, and because I am Yours, I can forgive -blank- for what they did. The words can be changed, but this gives you an idea of what to say."

She ripped out the paper, handed it to me, and put everything back in her purse. I folded it up and stuck it in my pocket. Then I stood up and looked out toward the water. She stood up beside me, and we looked at each other.

"Guess it's time to go."

"Yes, it's time to begin your new life. I'm so happy for you, Kessum. Please keep coming to church on Wednesday nights. If you do, you'll learn so much about Jesus."

"I'll be there."

CHAPTER FIVE

Christmas break would be the first time Shane and I had been together in over three weeks. With the rush of the season, finals, and Christmas parties, he didn't have time to come to Biloxi. Even though I'd been busy, I made time for him. I kept making plans, but one by one, they fell apart. Instead of being upset with my fiancé, I spent the extra time preparing for our wedding, shopping for presents, and decorating the cabin for the holidays.

Suddenly, one day, I heard his voice. He walked into the cabin singing 'I Wish You a Merry Christmas' with flowers in hand. Shane was grinning from ear to ear while he sang in his best Elvis impersonation. I quickly rinsed my soapy hands, turning off the water while wiping them on my shirt. He handed me the bouquet while he was still singing. I sat them down on the counter, leaning into his arms. When he finally let me go, we shared a long kiss before sitting down on the barstools.

"Why didn't you tell me you'd be here today?"

His grin turned into a big smile, showing those perfect white teeth. He reached over, taking my hand, saying, "Then it wouldn't have been a surprise, would it?"

"There's mischief in those green eyes of yours, mister. What's going on?"

His face flushed as he began to laugh nervously, then took me into his arms, burying his face in the curve of my neck. "I haven't done anything, and I'm not planning anything. I just wanted to surprise you and spend a little time together before they know I'm in town."

His embrace was tight, so I shifted, asking, "So your mom is expecting you?"

"Well, yes, it's Christmas time, right?"

"Nine more days."

"What do you want this year? A new yacht, private jet, or a Lamborghini?"

"Come on, Shane," I pouted, "you know I want all three. We would look so good on a yacht, having a party with twenty of our closest friends."

"Yes, we would, baby. Nothing but the best for Kessum Christy Williams."

"Whoa, I like the sound of that! Oh, and we could go any-where we want in your private jet. You name the country, and off we'll go. Just you and me, not any of our friends."

His arms wrapped tighter around my waist as he whispered, "We could join that club. The high-mile club, whatever it's called."

"Shane! Only after we're married, if your mom has anything to say about it."

"Our jet, our rules." Shane released his arms, and I reached for the bouquet. He sat back down, watching me search through the cabinets.

"We forgot about the Lamborghini!"

"Dang Kessum, you almost made me fall off this barstool."

"Sorry, did I say that too loud? I got a little excited about the car. What color would it be?"

"Hmm, I like white, but you'd probably look better in red."

"Why do you say that?"

"Because of that beautiful strawberry blonde hair, and red is your favorite color."

"You're right, and if you want to drive one, you'll have to buy another one, because you're not driving mine."

"Are you kidding me? I buy you a car, but you won't let me drive it?"

"Nope. You're not driving my Lamborghini, mister."

"Baby, you're going to change your mind, or I won't stop kissing you, ever."

"That much kissing could lead to a whole lot of trouble."

"That's the kind of trouble I need," Shane almost whispered before touching his lips to mine.

Each kiss washed away my doubts. His right hand pressed the small of my back, pulling me closer. My thoughts became lost in the smell of his cologne and his lips against mine.

"Wait, did you hear that?"

"Are you expecting someone?" Shane asked, looking at the front door.

"No, I don't know who it could be."

"I'll go see," he said, walking to the door slowly.

I found a green vase, filled it with water, and placed the flowers inside before setting it on the counter. Voices drifted toward the kitchen, so I went to see who was there.

Shane smiled and said, "Look who found me."

"Wow! He's only been here for a few minutes. Please come on in."

"Thank you so much, but we're not going to stay. I saw Shane's car and had to stop and say hello. I hope you don't mind."

"Of course not. This is your house. I wish you and Tyler would stay, Annie."

"We just have too much to get done today, Kessum. Maybe next time."

Mom, I'll walk you to your car." Shane stepped forward, then turned back, touching my arm before giving me a wink. Annie walked beside him down the steps before glancing over her shoulder to say goodbye.

It was only a moment—a Mom walking with her son. Somehow, I knew it would be one of those moments I'd never forget. There were certain things about my future mother-in-law that I didn't understand. However, her love for Shane and my love for him became our common bond. It would never break, no matter what happened.

The next day, we rushed toward the holiday season with determination. We would experience it all—the shopping, wrapping, dinner parties, Christmas parties, and seeing family and friends. Nothing could stop us from having it all, even though we only had a few weeks together.

The entire holiday season is my absolute favorite time of the year, and because of this, Shane did everything he could to make it merry. He knew my family didn't celebrate like his family when I was a kid. We didn't have a giant tree, lots of presents, or a party.

Because of this, he went overboard decorating the cabin. Under the tree were too many gifts to count, and he even surprised me on Christmas Eve by dressing up like Santa.

My future in-laws still outdid their son's efforts by having the best of everything. The big house was decorated as if it were the set of a Hollywood movie about Christmas. They wore the finest clothes, ate the best foods, and had decadent desserts daily. At their elaborate holiday party, where only the most important people were invited, they had endless champagne and expensive hors d'oeuvres. On Christmas Day, they exchanged expensive gifts beside a 12-foot-tall, winter-wonderland-decorated tree in matching pajamas. Honestly, it was a little over the top, but it was one of the best Christmases of my life.

New Year's Eve brought an even larger crowd to the big house. Annie and Arthur knew how to throw a party, and this one did not disappoint. Only the best food, champagne, and people were allowed. It was a black tie and evening gown event. Waiters carrying trays of beautiful hors d'oeuvres kept emerging from the kitchen. It was the kind of party everyone dreams of attending on New Year's.

After the countdown to midnight ended and the kisses were kissed, we all went outside. In the coolness of the night, beside the pool, fireworks began shooting from a nearby location into our view. Red, yellow, blue, and purple, with gold and silver sparkles, exploded with the crowd's approval.

Shane held me close as we watched the fireworks explode, sending an array of colors into the night sky. It felt like the beginning of everything I'd been dreaming about since I was a little girl. This year, I will be a bride and become a wife to the man I love. Soon we would have a new home and begin our own family. In his arms, I couldn't have been happier or more ready for our future together.

The days after New Year's and before Shane left for Hattiesburg were full of expectations. We went over the wedding plans, the venue, the guest list, and the food. Shane and I drove around the streets of Biloxi, trying to decide where we wanted our wedding announcement photos taken. We discussed possible honeymoon destinations with their family travel agent. We also talked about how we wanted our lives to be once we were married.

The evening before Shane had to leave for Hattiesburg, he stood at the window, staring out toward the lake. I sat on the couch, watching him. He pulled the curtain back further, looking down, asking, "Hey, do you remember the night we hid in the storm shelter from the cops?"

"Yes, of course I do."

He turned toward me, saying, "I feel like hiding again."

I walked to him as his eyes filled with tears. Shane wrapped his arms around me, pulling me close. I could feel his heart racing, and for a few moments, I felt emotional.

"You don't have to leave if you don't want to."

"I don't want to," he whispered.

"Then don't. You don't need a business degree to run a restaurant."

"They won't give me the restaurant unless I finish college. And if we don't have the restaurant, I need a degree. To get a good job and take care of our family."

"Our family? Are you already thinking about kids? We aren't even married yet."

Shane let go and turned back toward the window. I stood behind him and put my arms around his waist.

"Kessum, you know I want kids. Why are you asking me that?"

"I'm sorry. I didn't mean to upset you."

"It's just… my classes this semester will be hard. Then there's you. I don't know what you do with your time when I'm gone."

"I go to lunch with your Mom, and I'm planning this huge wedding. Oh, I go to church, too."

He took my hands, moved them, and walked to the back door. He opened it without a word and walked down the steps. The cold winter air rushed through the open door, and I went to close it. Then I saw him. He opened the storm shelter. I ran down the steps to go with him.

We stood in the cold, damp darkness until he found matches and lit a candle. Then he said, "Sometimes I wonder what would've happened if I hadn't kissed you that night."

"I don't know."

"That's because you never thought about kissing me, did you?" He asked, reaching for my hand.

"Back then, I thought about kissing everybody. I just wanted to be kissed…"

He reached up and took a plastic container off the shelf. Shane took out a blanket, spread it on the bed, and motioned for me to sit. Then he knelt in front of me with tears in his eyes again, barely able to say, "Kessum, I'm so sorry."

"What's wrong, my love?"

"I haven't done everything right, Kessum, but I love you. I never want to lose you."

"You can't lose me."

"I don't want to be like my dad or some of the other men I know," he said, burying his head in my lap.

"Shane, I'm not sure what you mean."

"I want to be a faithful man. Let's grow old together, for real. I'll still want to be with you when we're old."

"Where's all this coming from?"

"I'm sorry. I love you and don't want anybody else. I don't want to lose you. Let's make a vow to each other right now. God can be our witness."

"Shane?"

"You don't know how much it would mean to me. Don't you want to do it?"

"I think we could find a much nicer place if we're going to vow to God."

"Okay," he said, standing up and reaching out his hand for mine.

"Where do you want to go?" I asked, trying to understand his urgency.

"I'm not sure... but I know I don't want to go to Hattiesburg."

"It won't be long, and you'll be graduating. Then we'll be together every day."

"I know. Where do you want to be? If it weren't so cold, I'd say out by the water."

"Shane, I'm going into that warm cabin when I climb that ladder. You can decide where we should go. I don't care if it's your mom's house, the mall, or wherever, just somewhere warmer."

"Kessum, no matter what, I just want you to remember you mean everything to me. It's you and me, me and you, no matter what happens in this life. We'll always be together, in the good days and bad… best friends, business partners, and one day soon, Mom and Dad."

"So let me get this straight. You want to marry me, *you are deeply in love with me,* and you never want to live without me. Is that what I'm hearing, Mr. Williams?"

"Yes, that's what you're hearing, Mrs. Williams."

"I love it! And I love you so much. You can't even comprehend how in love with you I am right now."

We climbed the stairs to the cabin. When I reached for the doorknob, he pulled me back, kissing my neck. "I miss being here with you at the cabin."

"There have been so many times I stood in this spot and longed to feel your arms around me."

"How many times?"

"Every day, Shane, every single day. I've kept myself busy, going to church, learning about God, and how to be a good wife for you and a good mother to our children. Still, I missed you every day."

"You will be a good wife and mother. I hope to be a good husband and father, but it's harder for me than you know. My dad has had more *friend girls* than I can count. Of course, most people don't know that because Mom makes him keep them somewhere far away from Biloxi."

"We don't have to be like our parents or repeat their mistakes. We have our own lives, separate from Annie and Arthur or Pam and Richard. We can have a good marriage. It can't be that hard to love one another, take care of each other, and stay in love."

"We don't have to be anywhere special; let's do it right now. Kessum, I vow before God to take care of you, to guard your heart, to always love you, no matter what," he said, taking my hand, putting it on his chest.

"Shane, you are the only person I've ever loved. I vow before you and God that you will be my first and last love. I'm always going to believe in you. It's you and me forever and ever."

"Can we seal it with a kiss?" he asked, pulling me close. His lips touched mine, and everything else faded into the background. Suddenly, nothing else mattered—not the past, not the future, only this moment.

The hours and minutes we had left together flew by like dust flying off tires on a dirt road. Family dinners and wedding planning took up most of our precious time. Shane and I stole any moment we could to be alone. Sometimes it was for a walk and other times for a long drive.

With the rising of the sun on a cool January morning, it was time for Shane to leave. He put the last things he needed from the cabin in the car. I watched him load everything into the trunk from the front steps. When he turned to look back, he half walked, half ran, as I rushed down the steps to jump into his arms.

"Kessum, please don't make it any harder for me to leave."

"Shane, let's not say goodbye, just see you later."

"See you later, Mrs. Williams."

"See you soon, Mr. Williams. I love you."

He stood by the car, moving his head slowly from side to side, then stopped to say, "You'll be here when I get back."

"I'll be here," I nodded.

Shane stepped back, watching me. Then he got in the car. As the engine turned over, he opened the door, walking back toward the cabin. In a hurried rush, he kissed me, then whispered, I love you. He ran back, jumping in the driver's seat. Shane never looked back, not even for a second, before driving away.

The car became smaller as I watched him drive down the street. He didn't use his blinker before making the right-hand turn that would ultimately take him back to Hattiesburg. Being reasonable had never been something I was good at, so I called him.

"Miss me already?" Shane asked without saying hello.

"No, I don't miss you at all," I said, trying to hide my tears.

"I'm coming back."

"Right now?"

"Kessum..."

"I know you have to leave. I just wanted to say I love you one more time. And I forgot to tell you to call me when you get there."

Shane hesitated, then cleared his throat, saying, "Sorry, I'm getting into heavy traffic. Monday morning rush hour, I guess. I love you, too. I'll call. Now relax, take a long, hot bubble bath or something."

"Okay, please be careful."

"Will do. Bye."

"Bye," I said, debating whether to say I love you again, but then I heard him hang up.

He was right. A long, hot bubble bath was just what I needed. With soft music and a bath pillow, I almost fell asleep in the tub. When I finally got out, my fingers and toes were shriveled up. Not wanting to disturb the peacefulness, I took my time, drying off and getting dressed. Then I went to the kitchen to cook something to eat.

Spaghetti was the easiest thing to make from the ingredients I had. Of course, all that was in the cabinet was a jar of plain sauce. I added as many vegetables and spices as possible to enhance the flavor. A small piece of French bread was left over from a few days ago, and I covered it in butter and garlic. Once everything was ready, I sat down in front of the television and turned on a movie.

When the movie ended, I realized it was late afternoon, and Shane hadn't called. I picked up my phone to check and make sure I didn't miss his call, but nothing. There were no missed calls or messages. My first instinct was to call, but then I decided to wait. He was probably busy getting his things unloaded or grabbing a bite.

By six o'clock, it was dark outside, and I couldn't wait any longer to call. When I picked up the phone, I told myself to be calm, but I was already upset. What was he doing in Hattiesburg? I asked him to let me know when he'd made it there safely.

It rang and rang until it went to voicemail. Thirty minutes later, it was the same: no answer, no return call, no response to text messages. I didn't know what to do, so I called Trina, who told me I was overreacting. She made every excuse in the world for Shane, then told me to watch another movie and relax.

When I woke up on the couch the next morning, I practically jumped up and ran to the kitchen to check my phone. I couldn't believe my eyes when I realized the whole night passed without a single call or text from Shane. This time, I couldn't stop calling him over and over. I left voicemails until his mailbox was full. I sent so many text messages that I lost count.

Shane was unhappy about going back to Hattiesburg. He didn't want to leave me in Biloxi alone. We were both struggling to survive the separation of a long-distance relationship. With him ignoring me, I wondered if he wanted to tell me something I didn't want to hear. I kept running our last conversations through my mind, searching for a sign or clues for why he would treat me this way.

By mid-afternoon, I had spoken with the few friends I had in Hattiesburg. There were two guys and a girl we'd gone to high school with, and a couple of Shane's friends I'd met when I visited. No one had seen him. Most of them said I was probably worried for nothing. The only thing that made me feel better was when they agreed to look for him and let me know if they found him.

With nothing left to do except get in my car and drive to Hattiesburg, I picked up the phone to call his mom. Then I realized she would probably think we were in a fight and not do anything. Instead, I dialed Linda's number. I needed someone to talk to who wouldn't judge me. And she was one of the only people in Biloxi I could trust.

When Linda answered the phone, I asked if she could come over. She explained she was wrapping up her workday, which would take about an hour. However, when I began to cry, she said she'd get there as soon as possible.

The knock on the door startled me. Before I could answer, she knocked again. We barely sat down before it all came rushing out. What happened before and after Shane left, some of my fears, and a little anger.

"Shane didn't want to go to Hattiesburg, but he had to go."

"I know he didn't want to leave you. It's going to be okay, Kessum."

"I've called every person I know in Hattiesburg. Nobody has seen him. I don't know what else to do."

"Have you called Southern Miss?"

"I can't. We aren't related. They won't tell me anything about him," I replied, walking to the kitchen, then back to the couch.

"How long has it been since he left?" She asked, looking up at me, reaching for my hand.

"It's been one day, and almost six hours since Shane drove away," I replied, my anger turning back to concern.

Linda gently pulled my hand until I sat down beside her, then she said, "Kessum, you've waited long enough. You have to contact Shane's family."

"I'm going to call them, Linda."

"He should have returned your call or sent you a text by now."

"I know. And he's probably just busy or lost his phone or something."

Linda held my hand, then smiled before saying, "I'm worried about you. I know what you're going through; I've been there. One time, when I was younger, my boyfriend went on vacation to the Florida Keys. He promised to call me every day, but he didn't call me, not even once. They were gone for ten days. When he got home, he acted like he'd done nothing wrong. For ten days, I worried myself sick over him, and the whole time, he was hanging out at the beach with another girl, having fun."

"This is different, Linda. The man I'm about to marry isn't answering my calls. There's no excuse for the way he's treating me. I've put up with his mom, with a long-distance relationship, and wait! Do you think he's cheating on me?"

"Kessum, you need to calm down. Look, I know you're upset. You're probably having one hundred different thoughts with just as many emotions," she said, standing up, walking to the window, pulling back the curtain. The light from the sun streamed in from the window onto the floor.

"I'm praying Shane's okay, but it feels like God isn't listening."

"You are so fresh in your faith, like a baby."

"I know, but that doesn't help me."

"I'm sorry," she said softly, looking out the window. "You know I've always tried to be careful about giving advice."

"I know."

She walked to the couch and sat down, saying, "You know Jesus had a lot to say about forgiveness. As for me, one of the most powerful examples is the scriptures immediately following the Lord's Prayer in Matthew. Jesus said, and I'm paraphrasing, 'If you forgive men their trespasses, God will forgive you for yours. But if you don't forgive them, God will not forgive you.' Do you remember that one?"

"Yes, but does it mean that no matter what someone does, I'm supposed to forgive them?"

"Yes. It's not always easy, but that's what we're supposed to do. We cast all our cares on Jesus, and He takes care of us. Our cares could mean anything, including a fiancé who hasn't returned our calls."

"I forgive him. But I still want to drive to Hattiesburg and find him. Will you come with me?"

"Call his mom first and ask if she's heard from him."

"Okay, then what am I supposed to do, Linda? Sit by the phone? My heart is broken... I can't believe he's doing this to me."

She leaned closer, putting her arm around my shoulder. "I can't tell you what you should do, but I know what I do when I'm upset. I go to a place, my secret place, and I talk to Jesus. I tell Him everything, the good and the bad. Then, in my mind, I take all that stuff, that messy junk, and wrap it up in a blanket. Like a picnic blanket, you know, the blue and white plaid ones. Then I tie it up, put it in a big basket, and give it to God."

"Has God ever talked back to you?"

"He has, but not the way you're thinking. It's an inner voice or a feeling deep in my heart. Trust me, when God talks to you, you'll know it's Him."

"It's strange, Linda, but even talking about this has made me feel better."

"God is faithful, Kessum. He will meet you wherever you are and whatever season you're going through. Don't ever think you're alone. You are never alone, not even when you think you are. God is still there."

With those words and a hug, Linda gathered her things and left. The sun was slipping further down when I looked out the window to watch her drive away. My mind shifted through some of our conversation, leaving me wondering if she would go to Hattiesburg with me.

Then the more I thought about why Shane hadn't responded to my calls or texts, the more I wanted to cry. In a perfect world, I had done everything right. Annie insisted that I attend the First Baptist Church because she wanted her grandchildren to be raised in the church, so I went to church. Annie and Arthur didn't want me to work, so I stopped. Annie and Shane wanted us to have a huge wedding, so I dedicated myself to planning it.

Even though I was upset, I took Linda's advice. After swallowing my pride, I grabbed a flashlight and a jacket. Walking out the back door, I looked towards the lake. It was calm; the water looked almost like glass from a distance. As I got closer, the reflection of the trees and the most beautiful sunset lay upon the water's surface like an expensive oil painting. My heart felt sad as I gazed upon the beauty my eyes saw.

I closed my eyes; then I could see myself putting everything-Shane, his family, our wedding, my mom, and dad in that blue plaid picnic blanket. Tying up the edge of the blanket in my mind, I sensed someone was there. I looked to the left, spun around to look behind me, but nothing, no one. Closing my eyes, I put the blanket in a big wicker basket that I could see in my mind.

"I give it to You, Jesus. I'm sorry, it's too much. I don't want to carry it anymore."

A soft breeze lifted my hair. Then it felt like the weight on my shoulders became lighter. My eyes opened as leaves began wafting slowly down to the ground. Birds flew, landing in a nearby tree, and began to sing. My eyes searched the branches of the trees, trying to count them. At that very moment, I heard something I'd never heard before. It was like no man or woman's voice. It was like the voice of pure love that stirred my heart, made my body tingle. The voice dried my tears. This voice felt like it was wrapping me in the light of love while taking away that blanket full of hurt and sorrow. It was an unmistakable voice, but I didn't hear with my ears; it was a whisper from deep inside.

'You're okay, Kessum. I have you in the palm of My hand.'

CHAPTER SIX

Constantly checking my phone was not helping me at all. Without a call or message from Shane, I had no choice but to ask for help. Even though one hundred excuses and multiple scenarios entered my mind to explain why he hadn't called, my options were limited. I didn't want to worry his parents, but I knew they were probably the only ones who could do anything. If I called the police, I knew they wouldn't tell me anything since I'm only his fiancée. If I called the Mississippi Highway Patrol, they wouldn't give me any information either. Then I thought about filing a missing person's report, but I couldn't because we weren't married. I kept thinking about going to Hattiesburg, but I wouldn't know where to start looking for him, and I didn't want to go alone. If Shane were in the hospital, someone would have contacted his parents by now, and they would have contacted me.

Linda was right, so I picked up the phone and dialed the number. When she answered, I apologized, "Annie, I'm sorry to call so late."

"Kessum?"

"Yes, ma'am. Have you heard from Shane?"

"No. I intended to call you today, but I've been busy."

"I've been calling and sending messages."

"Kessum, stop crying. He's probably busy. I'll call him and call you back," Annie replied, hanging up without saying goodbye.

The tears I was trying to hold back would not stop falling. I reached over the edge of the bed, grabbing the Kleenex. Then I slid down the side of the bed onto the floor.

When the phone rang, I jumped up and rushed to the other side of the bed, asking, "Did he answer?"

"No, it went straight to voicemail, but the box is full."

"Before, it would ring, but now it's going straight to voicemail."

"Why didn't you call me sooner?"

"I didn't want you to be worried. I thought…"

"I'll call USM when they open in the morning, but I'm calling the police now. Did you call them yet?"

"No, I didn't think that I could."

"What about the hospitals?"

"No."

"Okay, I need to let you go."

"I didn't know what…"

There was no reason to finish the sentence. Annie hung up, not waiting to hear what I had to say. It was apparent to me now why I hadn't called. At the same time, it felt like I had done something wrong by not calling sooner.

On the other side of the bed, I knelt near the Kleenex. Pulling one, then two, I wiped my eyes dry of tears. Annie's tone kept running through my mind. Hints of shock and dismay, maybe even a bit of disappointment, came through in her tone. It felt like I was never good enough, no matter the situation, but especially in this one. The tears kept coming with no end in sight as I pulled another tissue from the box.

"God, I don't know You very well, but I know You know Shane. Please, God, let him be okay, even if he's doing something wrong or has decided he doesn't love me. I want him to be okay. If You could do that, God, I would be so thankful. Linda says to pray in Your son's name… in Jesus' name, God. I hope You hear me. I know I'm not good, like the people at church. I haven't read the Bible or done anything great for You, but I love Shane. No matter what happens, I want him to be okay. Please, God, let him be okay."

Crawling back on the bed, I lay down with a box of tissues and my phone beside me. I felt a little better after praying and calling Annie, even if she was upset. I opened the Photos app on my phone to look at pictures of Shane. The last picture we took was on New Year's Eve. We both looked so happy. It was taken right after we kissed at midnight.

Then I began to go back in time. Each picture tells a story, capturing a moment we would never relive. I always wanted to print copies of my favorites and make a photo album. A book to tell a little bit of our story, the beginning of our relationship.

Realizing there wasn't any reason to continue trying to contact Shane, I needed to keep my mind busy. I decided to create a one-of-a-kind gift for him. I went all the way back to the first picture we took together and began picking out the ones I wanted to put in a photo album.

Time lost its grip on me as I searched through 1,000 pictures, looking for the best of the best. Each picture deserving of a heart got one. As the number of my favorite pictures increased, a question came to mind. How many pictures did a photo album hold? I had never bought one before. I counted the pictures I had picked of the two of us, the places we've gone, and things we've done. Then, I searched for a photo album online.

There were huge ones, like some of the ones Mom keeps on our bookshelf at home. There were also little ones, big ones, thin ones, and fat ones. I never realized how many different photo albums were out there. You could get any color or size you can imagine. You could also have one custom-made. With unlimited options, it was hard to decide, but I knew I needed one to hold at least one hundred pictures.

It wouldn't be easy to narrow it down to one hundred, but that was exactly what I would do. The next time I saw Shane, I would have a meaningful gift to give him. Yes, I would probably be upset regardless of his excuse for not calling me. However, as I looked back on our memories, I knew that no matter what he had done, I wanted to spend the rest of my life with him.

After deciding to create the photo album, I felt a surge of energy. I rushed to the bathroom and started the shower. I turned on the music and got undressed as I sang The Middle by Zedd, Maren Morris, and Grey.

Stepping into the shower with the water rushing over my body, I felt revived. The shampoo poured out too quickly, but instead of being conservative and putting it back in the bottle, I put it on my head. I lathered up. Suds began to run down my shoulders and back. It didn't bother me; I just kept singing. Then I leaned my head back into the water and let it wash the shampoo away, along with the salty tears on my face.

When my mind drifted back to everything, to every reason I had to worry, I would turn it back to what I was trying to accomplish. I wasn't in a rush, but at the same time, I didn't take a long shower. I dressed, made the bed, and plugged my phone up to charge before cooking breakfast, eggs, toast, and grits. It was simple, easy, and one of Shane's favorites.

From the first bite to the last, I thought about giving the photo album to Shane. Thinking about him holding it, turning the pages, and looking at the pictures gave me more energy to stay positive. Usually, I never leave dirty dishes in the sink but today was different. I had something more important to accomplish than making sure the house was clean.

It was too cold to sit outside. I stayed at the kitchen table looking through the remainder of our pictures. When I moved to the living room to sit on the couch, there was a knock at the door.

"Just a minute," I said, trying to mentally note which picture and the number, knowing it was pointless.

"We didn't want to call," Annie said, walking in before I could answer the door with Arthur and Tyler.

"No, no, don't you dare say..."

With tears coming down her face, she opened her arms to embrace me, saying, "I don't want to tell you. Arthur..."

I crumbled down onto the floor, saying, "No, no, no, Arthur!"

"Kessum," he said, kneeling and wrapping his arms around me.

I pushed back, asking, "What happened? Where is he?"

"We didn't want you to be alone," Annie cried. She stepped closer, keeping her arm around Tyler.

Tears streamed down Tyler's face. He choked back the tears, saying, "I can't believe it; none of this seems real."

Looking at their faces, I didn't know how to react. It didn't make sense why they were not answering a simple question, so I asked again, "What happened to Shane?"

Arthur looked into my eyes, his full of tears, saying, "He's gone, sweetheart. I'm so sorry, but he's gone."

"What do you mean he's gone! I don't understand! Why are you saying that?"

Annie took my hand and said, "Come on, darling, I'll help you. Let's sit on the couch. Arthur, will you see if Richard and Pam are here?"

"Yes, I'll… wait outside for them to get here. Tyler, do you want to stay here with your mom, or do you want to come with me?"

"I'm coming with you, Dad."

Annie put her arm around my shoulder. We walked side by side back to the couch. My phone was on the armrest, and for a second, I thought about our pictures. My mind felt like it was in a dense fog. The words, he's gone, he's gone kept rolling like a wave crashing over my entire body.

"Kessum," Annie whispered. "Are you okay? You feel so cold. Let me, let me get a blanket."

"I've been going through all our pictures this morning. I was going to surprise him with a photo album. I just wanted to do something…"

"You're going to be okay. We're going to get through this together. My son loved you. I'm sorry… I didn't realize…"

"He still loves me!"

"That's my son, such a good boy."

"No, Annie! Oh my God! NO!"

"It's okay, shhhh…"

"Please, please tell me I'm dreaming. Oh God, please…"

"It was just his time; it was Shane's time to go to heaven."

"Why? Why would God do this to me?"

Annie didn't answer. Instead, she got up and went to get the box of tissues. Putting them down beside me, she went to the kitchen. Not a single tear fell until she walked away. Then an unending flow of tears fell down onto my cheeks and neck.

Annie placed two glasses of water on the coffee table, pulled tissues out of the box, and then sat back down. I demanded, "Annie, tell me it's not true! He's at college; he's just been busy."

"No, Kessum. It started raining when Shane was going back to USM. His car left Highway 49, and they just found him this morning. They believe he died on impact, but there's no way to know."

"It's my fault. I knew when he didn't call me that something might be wrong. I didn't want to bother you or Arthur. I just thought Shane was tired and probably unpacked his car and went to sleep. You know he didn't even want to go back to Hattiesburg."

"It's not your fault! I never want to hear you blame yourself again. Yes, when you didn't hear anything, you should have called. Now, all of that is in the past. Let it go. I have to do the same. My son passed away, and I didn't even call him once to make sure he made it safely."

"Annie, it's not your fault either," I said, touching her arm.

"I never said the accident was my fault. I said I never called or messaged to check if he made it to Hattiesburg safely. I just thought you would do that."

The door opened, and we turned to see who was coming. Annie got up as Mom rushed in, taking Annie's seat. Dad walked to the other side, pushed back the coffee table, and knelt. Without a word, they both embraced me and held me while we cried.

CHAPTER SEVEN

After packing everything I owned in cardboard boxes, I opened the back door and walked down the steps. It was the middle of June. The high humidity of a Mississippi summer made it hard to breathe. Birds sang their songs as a hot breeze rustled the leaves on the trees. I walked down to the water's edge and looked across Big Lake. Memories flooded my mind as I wondered why Shane had to die so young. Everyone kept telling me to let it go and focus on the future, but that was easier said than done.

The heat was terrible, but I tried not to think about it. Instead, I thought about Shane. I thought about the special moments we shared here together. I thought about the fun we shared with our friends at this lake. It felt like a lifetime since we were standing together at this very spot. The sadness deep within me began to surface again. It existed right below the top layer of skin. It was always right there; it didn't matter how hard I pushed it down.

It wouldn't be long before Mom and Dad would knock on the front door. Then I would leave this place, which holds so many memories that Shane and I shared. It wasn't my decision to leave. It was made by people who say they have my best interests in mind. I wasn't sure about that, but when Annie and Arthur asked me to move out of the cabin, I had questions I never asked.

Walking back towards the house, the little door of the storm shelter stood out. I had to go there one last time. The hinges creaked as I pulled on the handle. The smell was the same, damp dirt. Nothing had changed since the last time Shane and I descended those steps. The blanket he had laid on the bed not so long ago was still there when he told me he didn't want to leave. Then I remembered the vow he was desperate to make before he left. I closed my eyes, cleared my mind, and took myself back in time to our first kiss.

Now, as I stood in the storm shelter, I could see things much more clearly. I had nothing to look forward to... no wedding, marriage, husband, or children. It felt like I was in a foreign land. I couldn't speak the language, I didn't know the customs, and I didn't know how to get back home. The worst part about it was that I was utterly and completely alone with nothing but memories.

As I climbed the steps, I thought about my relationship with Shane's family. It was strained during the best times and almost nonexistent at others—the many reasons why are buried beneath the mourning heart of his mom. Why I thought Annie would want me to remain in their lives seemed ridiculous now. Ultimately, the ties that could have bound us did not exist, not even our shared love for Shane.

Mom and Dad didn't know what to do in this situation. Neither did I. When I left home, they had continued their lives as I had begun mine. By this time, they probably expected I would be settled down. They would have a son-in-law from a good family, and their daughter would have her own life. Now, I couldn't see myself being someone else's wife, much less having someone else's children.

With the truck loaded, we drove to my childhood home. Dad insisted that Mom and I go in and relax because he had someone coming to help him unload everything. My argument was met with a resounding no, so I went inside and sat at the kitchen table.

It felt like I'd taken a step back in time. Nothing had changed. The same pictures hung on the wall, the same old furniture sat in the same place, and the same decorations were on the kitchen table.

Mom went to the refrigerator and brought back two bottles of sweet tea. The caps were tight, so she handed them to me. When it was hard for me, I picked up a cloth napkin to help me get a good grip, but she stopped me. How quickly I had forgotten her many rules. She handed me a paper towel and nodded with that same look on her face that I remembered so well.

"Where do you want me to put this one, Mr. Howards?"

"Cooley, is that you?"

"Yep, it's me. I'm here to help your dad. Well, I'm helping you, but he's the one who asked," he said, setting the box down, opening his arms.

"I'm so glad to see you," I replied, hugging him tightly. Even though I tried to hold it in, tears began to fall.

"Good to see you. It's been too long," he replied, as I buried my face in his shirt.

I leaned back, looking at him, and apologized, "I'm sorry. I try, but sometimes I just can't."

"You don't have to apologize to me, Kessum. I miss Shane, too," he consoled, hugging me tighter.

Mom whispered, "You need to let Cooley get back to work before your dad hurts himself."

"Hello, Mrs. Howards. How are you today?"

"Fine. My daughter and I were having some sweet tea. I have a bottle for you when you're finished."

"Sounds good," Cooley said, hugging me closer before he let go.

"Mom, do you have any tissues?"

"Here's a napkin."

Being back at my parents' house shook me to the core. Reality sank in when I stepped inside and knew I had nowhere else to go. I told myself this was my home, but I knew it wasn't my home anymore. Truth be told, I didn't have a home. This was just a visit, a pitstop to only God knows where. How I ended up here made me want to cry even more. All the hopes and dreams for my future were invested in a boy I loved more than myself. Now, he is gone, and with him, all my hopes and dreams have died.

Cooley finished helping Dad and sat beside me at the kitchen table. The conversation between the four of us felt awkward. Every time he or I brought up Shane, Mom changed the subject. It felt like we were little children talking about something we shouldn't.

"Thanks for the tea, Mrs. Howards. I have to get going. I've got other things to take care of before it gets dark," Cooley said, standing up, extending his hand toward Dad.

"Thanks for your help," Dad said, shaking his hand.

"Not a problem. If you need help with anything else, Mr. Howards, just let me know."

"I'll walk you out," I said, standing up, pushing the kitchen chair under the table.

We walked out to his truck, and he opened the door before he turned to ask, "How are you doing?"

"Not good. I feel completely lost, like I don't know what to do. I've never felt this alone in my entire life."

"Losing Shane is hard on me, and we hadn't been that close lately. You know I'm here if you want somebody to talk to," he said, reaching for my hand.

"I know. I should've already called you. It feels like I've been in a storm and can't find my way out. Shane has been gone for months, but most of the time, it feels like just a few days, or hours, sometimes like minutes, then at other times... forever."

"It's hard to move on, but it's something you have to do. Have you thought about what might have happened if you had left with me that night?"

"I wouldn't have been arrested."

"No, you wouldn't have, and you wouldn't have a record."

"I don't know why I didn't leave with you that night."

"I think you were worried about Tommy and Sarah," Cooley replied, turning to look at the house but not letting go of my hand.

"You're probably right, but if I had left with you, my life would have been a lot different."

"It's crazy how the littlest decisions impact so many lives. Do you know you broke my heart that night? The next day when Shane was talking about you. I was so mad at him."

"I didn't know, Cooley. Why didn't you ever tell me?"

"I figured you'd know. I thought you could tell by the way I acted after you and Shane got together," he explained, looking into my eyes.

"I never meant to hurt you. You're one of my favorite ex-boy-friends, not that I have too many."

"I guess it's all in the past now. And it's not easy to say, but that's how you'll have to think about Shane. It's what I'm trying to do, too. It's hard to believe I'll never see his face or shake his hand again."

"I'm trying, but it's so hard," I said, looking down at the ground.

"Thank God you don't have to do it alone," he said, squeezing my hand.

"I have nothing to thank God for at this point in my life. This wouldn't have happened if He loved me as much as people tell me He loves me. How people can think a 'loving God' sitting up there in the clouds could let my love, my life, die in a car crash is something I'll never understand."

"Don't ask me to defend God. You know it says His ways are beyond our understanding. But I know there is a God, and I'm pretty sure He didn't have anything to do with Shane having a wreck."

"He could have stopped it. He could have protected him."

"Kessum, if there's anything I know, and you know I don't claim to know much… being angry at God will not help you."

He climbed into the truck and waited for me to respond. My emotions swirled like the wind in a hurricane. I was torn between yelling at him and crying. Deep within my gut, I argued with myself that he was the last person on Earth who should be talking to me about God. Somewhere in the jumbled mess of my heart, I knew he was trying to help.

"Cooley, I know it's not good to be angry at God. It's just going to take time for me to figure this out. Until then, I don't even want to think about God or those holier-than-thou church people who don't have any answers. I'm done with that situation for… maybe forever."

"Everybody has to make their own choice when it comes to God. To believe in Him or not to believe in Him. You know I'm just one of those good old southern boys. I drive a truck and wear cowboy boots. I like cornbread and turnip greens, and I love Jesus. That's just the way I was raised."

"I was raised differently. Mom and Dad are about to get a second chance, I guess," I said, stepping back.

"I don't see you staying here long. Probably just a few months until you decide what you want to do. Hope you know you can come and see me anytime. You can even spend the night if you want to. We have an extra bedroom."

"I'm sorry, I'm drawing a blank on your girlfriend's name."

"Tammy Settles, not Tammy Wynette, but she does look like her," he said, smiling, then winking.

"I don't know what Tammy Wynette looks like, but your girl-friend is pretty. I met her at the funeral."

"She's pretty, but not as pretty as you. Your kind of pretty goes all the way from the outside down into your bones."

"Thanks," I replied, looking down at my bare feet.

"Hey, believe it or not, you still have a good life ahead. Any man would be blessed to have you as their girl. I know God has something great in store for your future."

"Until then, I'm going to my childhood bedroom to unpack. Don't be surprised when you get a phone call or knock on your door in a few days and it's me."

"I'll let Tammy know, and we'll be expecting you," he said, cranking the engine. He closed the door and then put the window down. "I'd better hear from you soon."

"I'll come see you soon."

Cooley backed out of the driveway, waving goodbye. I watched until his truck got smaller and smaller, and I couldn't see it. He had to go home to his girlfriend, but I wished he could have stayed longer.

As I walked back toward the front door, I smiled. Cooley had made me feel like one day I might be happy again. I caught a glimpse of what could happen somewhere in the distant future. Maybe not the whole husband and children thing, but me living my life. Not depressed or in mourning but simply having a job and a place of my own.

The moment I began to picture the future, guilt flooded my thoughts. They dampened my one tiny spark of hope until it was gone. It was the same feeling that kept me from everything. It was the guilty feeling that if Shane couldn't work or fulfill his dreams, then why should I? After all, it was my fault. I didn't care enough about him to pick up a phone when he needed help. Ultimately, I was the one who left Shane alone in that car to die.

CHAPTER EIGHT

They say it gets easier as time passes. Time had been passing- a massive river of time since the last time I looked into Shane's eyes. By now, I thought things would be different, but change wasn't easy for me. If I could say there was an easy part, it would be when I was sleeping. Waking up was the worst part of living without Shane. Every morning before opening my eyes, I remembered he was gone… forever. No matter how much I wanted to see him, I knew it would never happen unless it were in a dream. Then I went through the questions, which led to guilt. Every day, every morning, my heart felt the pain of not making a call or doing whatever I had to do to find him.

My parents took me in, sheltering me from the world for 15 months. We braved the worst of the COVID-19 pandemic together. We invented ways to spend our time at home while rebuilding family bridges. Mom and I learned how to do oil painting, concocted more family recipes, and played board games with Dad. Almost every week, he bought new books for our growing library. The books helped more than anything to keep my mind off the future. A future in which I couldn't see anything I wanted happening.

Home held a new meaning now that I had spent so much time there. Dad was still the same. He kept to himself, always busy with the next project. Mom, however, was different now. I couldn't pinpoint exactly how she changed. Even the way she dressed and her tone of voice had softened. Maybe it was a little bit of everything: Shane's sudden death, the pandemic, and being home more than usual.

Before, when I'd dropped out of school and left home, I hardly thought about either of my parents. All I thought about was myself and what I wanted or didn't want to do. Now it was easy to see how selfish, how unforgiving I'd been to my parents. After all, they were just people doing their best to take care of me.

Mom corrected me in the past because she wanted to protect me. She tried to guide me away from the bad and toward what was good. If I hadn't been so hardheaded, my life would have gone in a different direction. Chances are, Shane and I would never have dated, much less been engaged. If I had listened to my mom and dad, there would be a chance he'd still be alive.

The truth is that I was a typical teenager, and I thought I knew everything. I didn't want my parents to tell me what to do. Over the last few months, I realized how wrong I had been about them. Now, I know how much they love me and only want the best for my life.

It was time for me to get back to living and planning for my future. No, it would never be exactly how I wanted or thought it would be. It was something I'd come to terms with and moved forward as best I could. Sometimes I felt like I had done exactly that… moved forward. Other times, it was a day-by-day process of letting go of the past and focusing on the future.

Waitressing was the only job I'd ever had, so I applied at nearly every good restaurant on the Mississippi Gulf Coast. It took a while, but I finally went to work at Mary Mahoney's Old French House. If I said I was surprised, that would be an understatement. Waitressing jobs at Mary Mahoney's were hard to get. After thinking about it, I probably got the job because of Annie and Arthur. They must have put in a good word for me.

Working helped fill my time and gave me something to focus on instead of myself. The people I worked with became my new friends, whom I was thankful to have. Even a few of my old customers remembered me from Arthur's restaurant. Then, after a few months of waitressing, I signed a lease on my first apartment. It was nothing fancy, just a small one-bedroom and close to work.

The car was loaded with everything I owned before I hugged my parents goodbye. The apartment building wasn't too far from home. They both offered to come and help unload the car, but I told them I wanted to do it myself.

As I drove the car around the two-story, red-brick building, I felt a tingle of excitement. The steps up to the apartment reminded me of the steps in the stairwell at Biloxi High School, all steel and concrete. The little apartment was empty; only my voice echoed as I said out loud to no one, I'm home.

After climbing those stairs for what felt like one hundred times, I sat on the living room floor, surrounded by boxes and bags. The blinds in the living room were halfway drawn, and from where I was sitting, I could see a small playground. There was a little girl who couldn't have been more than five playing with her mom. At first, watching her play brought a smile to my face. Then, out of nowhere, the tears began to fall. Even after all this time, I never knew what would make me feel empty or sad.

The same question of why kept running through my mind day after day. I'd tried many ways to stop it, but it was always there. Today, of all days, when I should be happy at what I'd accomplished, I couldn't stop asking myself why. Why me, God? Why did this have to happen to us? Why did you take Shane away from me, God?

For the second time during my life, I heard a voice whisper, '*I have you in the palm of My hand.*'

"How can I believe it? How can You have me in the palm of Your hand when my life is messed up? It's a total train wreck! Can't you see me? I'm barely hanging on. It's my fault, and everybody knows it. I wish it had been me in that car instead of Shane. He had everything to live for, and I have nothing!"

Silence never seemed so silent as after I said- I have nothing. Tears, which once fell freely, quickly dried up. It was as though my anger and desperation shifted the atmosphere. I listened, but there were no sounds, no reply, and no one knocked on the door.

Scooting across the floor, I used the first garbage bag filled with clothes as a pillow. The ceiling was white with little swirly designs. My eyes followed the swirls from one side of the living room to the other. My stomach growled loudly, so I turned onto my side, looking toward the kitchen. The refrigerator was empty, and I knew it was empty, but still, I imagined something good was inside.

Without unpacking a thing, I grabbed the keys and my purse and walked out the door. It was time to get something to eat. I walked downstairs, remembering something a customer once told me. I can't remember his name anymore, but I knew I needed to adopt his perspective if I could.

He had lost someone he loved and found it hard to go on with life. It took time, but when his sadness ended, he started living life more purposefully. He explained that the person he loved could not do the things they wanted to do on this Earth. In their honor, he traveled the world, went to museums, attended concerts, and spoke with people from different countries and beliefs. To him, the part of the person he lost, that lived within his heart, lived on through him in everything he did and experienced. This allowed him to live in peace and experience life more fully, although he still missed his loved one.

I walked down the stairs and heard a familiar voice. "Linda, what a surprise."

She opened her arms and smiled. "It's been too long, Kessum. I thought I'd bring you a housewarming gift. It's in the car."

"You didn't have to do that."

"I know, but I wanted to see you. Your first apartment. You must be excited."

"I wouldn't exactly call it excited, but…" I shrugged, following her to the car.

"Now I feel like I've interrupted you. Were you going somewhere?"

"To grab a burger or something. There's nothing here to eat."

"You look like you're not eating at all. I know it's hard, honey, but you have to eat."

"I know. I promise I'll do better."

"You're skinny as a rail. And your color… well, I'm sorry I shouldn't say anything, but I'm worried about you, Kessum."

"I just don't have an appetite."

"Lord knows my husband wishes I'd lose some of mine," she replied, touching her belly.

"I don't think he'd want you to lose him to lose your appetite. I'm sorry I didn't…"

"There I go again, I'm sorry. You're going to be okay; things will get better."

"That's what everybody says, but I'm not sure. Most days, I would rather lie in bed and not do anything."

"Have you talked to anyone about how you're feeling?"

"No, I haven't. I'm too busy trying to get myself together."

Linda turned, put her hand on my arm, saying, "Well, you're not gonna believe what I brought you."

"Um, I'm guessing it's food."

"Yes, food, along with a few other things. I didn't know if you were having a housewarming party."

"Haven't thought about having a housewarming party. But now that you said it, that's not a bad idea. I was just about to get something to eat, then go shopping."

"Well, now you have plenty to eat. I brought the staples-milk, bread, and butter. Oh, and I baked you a chicken casserole, made a salad, and brought you yeast rolls, along with a loaf of banana bread. I know how much you like it," Linda said, picking up a large shopping bag.

"Thank you so much, Linda. This is so nice of you. Mom and I did a lot more cooking during the pandemic, and I learned a lot."

"We have all become better cooks and probably ate too much lately."

"Do you want me to carry that other bag? These steps are steep; I don't want you to fall."

"If you don't mind," Linda replied, handing me the smaller bag before we started up the stairs.

"Come on in and set it on the kitchen counter."

"Kessum, this apartment is so cute. Have you decided how you're decorating it?"

"Haven't got a clue. I've never had a place I needed to decorate. Here, let's put this in the fridge. I'll eat this later. I don't have plates, spoons, forks, or anything."

Linda put the casserole, milk, and salad in the refrigerator. Then, she unpacked another bag. It had a basket of fruit with two books.

"I didn't know if you had a copy of this, but it's called Jesus Calling. It's a daily devotional. Everyone at church loves this book. It's like Jesus is talking directly to you when you read it."

She handed me the little book. I glanced at it, then laid it down.

"This one," Linda said, holding the book up so I could see the cover, "No Wonder They Call Him the Savior by Max Lucado is one of my favorites. A friend gave it to me when I wasn't sure where I stood with God. You have to read Come Home. It's near the end. I put a bookmark where it begins for you. It's only three pages, but so powerful."

"Thanks. Since COVID, I've been reading more. I'll take a look when I get time."

"You know what, I'm hungry too. I could message Jordan and tell him we're going out to eat. I'm sure he wouldn't mind watching the boys tonight."

"We could, but I want you to know I'm not feeling very good before you call him. I don't want to hurt your feelings, but I don't want to talk about God or Jesus or anything to do with religion. If that's why you're here, then it's better if I go alone."

Linda paused, looking at me before saying, "I'm not here for any other reason than I love you. If I've talked about Jesus too much, I'm sorry. I never wanted to make you feel uncomfortable. It's hard not to talk about Him and what He's done in my life. You can't imagine what my life was like, what I was like before He saved me. Maybe one day I can tell you the whole story."

"I look forward to hearing your story but... just not today," I said, turning off the lights and walking out the door.

"I want to go with you if that's okay. We can take my car," she said, pulling her phone out as we started down the steps.

"That's okay; I can just meet you there. Remember, I have shopping to do?"

"Oh, that's right. Hey, we could talk about decorating ideas over dinner."

"Sounds like a plan. Where do you want to eat?" I asked before opening the car door.

"Wherever you want to go is fine with me. I'm following you."

Linda followed me to downtown Ocean Springs. We parked near the train tracks and walked down Washington Avenue. I had no idea where to eat. With various restaurants throughout downtown, I let her lead the way and figured we could pick one together. The narrow streets, full of cars, and the sidewalks crowded with people of all ages made me smile. The late afternoon sun made it feel more like spring than a November day.

Linda seemed happy, chatting about things she saw in shop windows that would be cute for my apartment. Her voice was full of hope. I desperately wanted to feel it, too, but I couldn't. Instead, my mind flooded with memories.

The first time Shane and I came here was on a sunny afternoon before we went to the beach. Another time, when we were here for the Art Walk, he bought me a beautiful painting of the lighthouse in Biloxi. Then, that overwhelming feeling gripped me again. It happened more than I told anyone. I saw someone who looked like him from a distance.

Since he passed away, my eyes constantly scanned faces whenever I was in a crowd. My heart never let me forget the color of his hair, the curve of his face. Whenever a guy with Shane's shade of hair and about his height was nearby, my heart skipped a beat.

I didn't know how to stop it or if it would ever stop. Why my mind continually played tricks on me didn't make sense. Shane was utterly gone and buried. There was no logical reason this kept happening to me. I was there when they closed his casket before moving it into the sanctuary at the funeral home. Still, I searched for his face everywhere I went.

CHAPTER NINE

Time, with its constant forward motion, filled my days with monotonous repetition. My mind preferred it that way. I rarely gave much thought to what needed to be done next. My spirit longed for more than continual tedious duties. The only part of me that won in this struggle was my heart. It demanded to be protected at all costs. It felt like it could only be kept safe if I continued doing the same things day after day.

Minutes before the alarm rang, I woke up right on time. The first thought to enter my mind was Shane, always Shane. It was becoming easier to push the thoughts away, to the back of my mind. Still, every morning, without fail, they were there, and there was little I could do to change it.

It was just a normal day, like all the others. Woke up, brushed my teeth, got dressed, ate breakfast, and went to work. Nothing unusual happened. No strange feelings or unusual thoughts entered my mind. It was just another day.

Had I not forgotten my phone, things might have been different. My internal clock sounded the alarm to hurry, or I'd be late. There were thirty-six steps up and thirty-six steps down before I could be on my way. If I was going to be on time, it was either hurry back upstairs or leave the phone.

Going upstairs was easy, other than catching my breath. With the keys still dangling in the lock, I searched the place without closing the door. It was on the arm of the couch, which was strange. Usually, I put the phone beside my keys on the kitchen counter.

The door closed harder than expected. Looking around, I checked to see if I'd disturbed anyone. My next-door neighbor opened his door. Not wanting him to get in front of me, I quickly stepped back, twisting the knob, making sure it was locked. Rushing to be first, I barely said hello before beginning the 36-step descent.

The sound of my steps in fast repetition caused a strange echo in the stairwell. My neighbor called after me, asking why I was in such a big hurry. For a moment, I thought about pretending not to hear him. Wasn't it obvious I didn't have time to talk? How many times had he seen me rushing to get to work?

With one glance at my phone to check the time, my eyes lost sight of the next step. The phone flew out of my hand as the sound of flesh and bones hitting metal steps filled the stairwell. Everything began to move in slow motion. My body was falling, but somehow, I felt separate from it. There was a part of me that knew what was happening and another part that felt like it wasn't happening to me. Then, without another thought, my world faded into darkness.

A massive wave of relief came over me when I stood up. My first thought was, how could I fall down the stairs like that and still be okay? My hands went directly to my head. Looking down at my hands, there was no sign of blood. I turned to look at my neighbor, Chance, to ask him if he'd seen me fall. That's when I saw myself, my body. It was broken, my leg at a peculiar angle and my left arm wedged behind my back. Chance knelt beside me, holding my right hand, calling for help.

It was hard to see myself this way. One of the neighbors opened her door and screamed when she saw me. Chance kept asking her to call 911, but she stood there crying. He saw my phone just a few feet from my body. He grabbed the phone and tried to open it, but he didn't know the passcode. He fell to his knees and leaned down where he could whisper in my ear. Tears fell from his eyes onto my face. I couldn't feel it, but I could still see them. Then he jumped up and ran up the stairs, into his apartment.

In the moments he was gone, I moved closer to myself. I didn't know what was happening or what to do. The only thing I knew was that I needed to get back inside my body. It felt strange, but I thought if I lay on top of myself, I would sink back in and be where I belong. When I did this, I didn't sink; it was like I floated just above. No matter how hard I tried, I couldn't get back inside. That's when I stood up. With a sense of urgency, I tried to jump back into my body. When it didn't work, I tried again. Jumping even higher with more force was unsuccessful, and then Chance came running back.

The ticking of the clock and its never-ending forward motion stopped. Time meant nothing. The man I lived beside for over a year, who tried so many times to have a conversation with me, sat on the ground, holding my bloody hand. Every word he said I heard, but he could not hear me. Screaming didn't change the fact that his ears were deaf to my pleading. When he started asking me to stay with him, that was the moment I realized I was dead.

If I could focus on his voice, not what was happening to me, I felt like I could stay. Now, I wanted to live, to get to know my neighbors, and be with friends and family. I didn't want to die. My whole life was ahead of me. There were still so many things to do and see. Now, I know we don't die when we leave our bodies. There's something else after this life.

The ambulance sirens alerted more people in the apartment complex, and they came to see what was happening. My downstairs neighbor was praying for me. Her voice was louder than anyone else's—but I knew she was fighting for my life.

The EMTs ran toward us. They asked everyone who was gathered around my body to move back. Even though they weren't talking to me, I moved closer to Chance. He was upset. Then I could see concern on several faces in the crowd. Why I never saw it, the compassion people have for each other when I was alive made me feel foolish.

When my body was loaded into the back of the ambulance, I stood and watched them close the door. The man quickly opened the driver's door, turning on the sirens. Without knowing what to do, whether to stay or go, I ran after the ambulance and jumped. It was my body. I needed to be close to it if I wanted to live.

In the back of the ambulance, a woman began to work to revive my body. She cut my clothes, gave me shots, and shocked my heart, but nothing was happening. Words came out of my mouth, but she could not hear them. Even though she didn't know me, she spoke like she did. She was trying to save my life in the only way she knew how. She was telling me to fight.

We arrived at the hospital, where a team was waiting. The moment the back doors of the ambulance opened, they rushed my broken body inside. Now, I floated higher from the floor than I wanted, but it was getting harder to resist the pulling sensation I felt. It was difficult to watch what they were doing to the body. However, I knew these people —people I didn't even know —might be my only chance of survival.

The chaos around me suddenly faded into the background as light poured into the room from the ceiling. I turned back to look at what the doctors and nurses were doing. Then, the light overcame everything in sight. No more people, no more voices, no more machines, no more walls, and no more hospital. All I could see was brilliant white light. All I could feel was its gentle pull on my spirit. It carried me up toward the ceiling, up through every floor in the hospital until I was above it. Even though I looked down, I was still rising. A part of me wanted to say no, let me stay. That part of me lost the battle as the light gathered me within itself and took me above the clouds.

My mind felt jumbled as fragments of sentences began with no ending. I was moving so fast that there was no time for questions and no time for answers. It felt like an eternity but could have been seconds, hours, or days while traveling in the light. All my life, time had ruled everything. Wherever I was, wherever I was going, was not ruled by time.

Pulling, floating, and gliding were the only things I felt. It was peaceful, more peaceful than I'd ever felt before. I didn't give a second thought to the body I'd left behind because I knew it wasn't me. There was no fear. I was alone, but I didn't feel alone. Nothing was around me, but everything surrounded me. Freedom was a word from Earth with many different meanings. It was only in this light that I understood what freedom meant. I never wanted it more, and now that I had it, I never wanted to leave.

My eyes caught a glimpse of something green in the distance. I knew it was where I was going, where I was meant to be. With just one thought, my direction turned, and the light carried me swiftly toward my destination. The closer I got, the greenness in everything my eyes could see became even more beautiful. The light carried me all the way, gradually expanding to the most amazing sight I had ever seen.

All motion stopped. I stood at the edge of a massive field of the most vibrantly alive, greenest green grass. On the left was a river. It wasn't like any river I'd ever seen on Earth. The water was like crystals, shining more glorious than diamonds in bright sunlight. There were gorgeous trees near the water's edge that were so perfect they didn't look real, but they were more real than anything I'd ever seen on Earth. Their leaves moved gently in the sweet-smelling wind. The grass, everything I could see, was full of light, full of life. Never had I felt more alive or seen anything more alive than what my eyes were now seeing.

A thought flashed in my mind that I could stand in this spot for the rest of eternity and be completely satisfied. If not for the tugging on my heart, that's exactly what I had decided to do.

The first few steps felt strange because my feet did not touch the ground. Instead, I was walking on top of the grass. It felt like I was floating or gliding. The energy, the light pulsating from the grass, flowed into the bottom of my feet and up through my legs. It was alive, and even though I had died, I was alive, more alive than I'd ever been before I came to this place.

When I saw Him, I knew He was the reason I was here. Waves of light emanated in every direction, brighter than the light coming from everything else. He sat on a large rock near the water's edge. His right hand was in the water, and His face looked down toward it. When I got closer, He turned to look at me. His eyes captured me, and I knew I was home.

Then, out of the field of green grass, a dog came running towards us. When the dog came closer, I couldn't believe what I saw. It looked just like Skipper, the little white and brown mixed-breed dog I had as a young girl. The dog went to Jesus, who gave it a pat on the head, and then it turned back to me.

Kneeling, I watched as it ran across the brilliant green grass. Could this be Skipper? The dog who had been my best friend for most of my childhood. He had been more than a dog to me. Skip was almost like a sibling because I didn't have one. He knew all my secrets, good and bad, and He still loved me.

In a display of light and sound, he approached slowly. I wasn't sure what was happening, but when the Skipper look-alike jumped into my arms, I checked for the unique red spot of hair on his chest. He let me hold him like a baby, just like he used to, and there it was, a tiny red splotch of hair. There was no denying it; I just knew it was him.

Skipper was happy, very much alive. I petted, hugged, and kissed him on his head like I did when I was a little girl. He squirmed, wiggled, and made funny little noises like he did back then. Being with my dog was like visiting an old friend you didn't realize you'd been missing.

All those times when I was little and felt like I knew what he was thinking, I now realize that was real. Because as I held him in my arms, I could hear his thoughts. Skipper kept repeating, 'I love you, I love you, I love you. I've missed you so much. I'm so glad you're here. I love you so much.' Then he jumped out of my arms, running towards the crystal river.

Once again, I was floating above the grass, being pulled towards the lover of my soul. Everything all around me pulsated with light and energy. There was a melody, a peaceful, calming song that was constantly playing yet always changing. It could have been chaotic, but the melody blended perfectly with the light. It felt like it was just under the surface of everything yet coming from everywhere. It was like the constant, harmonious humming of sounds from a waterfall, with soft voices in the distance. I understood little about what was happening, but as I moved closer to the river, I realized I didn't need to understand.

"Kessum," He said, arms stretched wide.

The eyes of Jesus looked like an ocean of love, electric and full of light. Liquid love flowed from His eyes into me, filling me with joy until it started pouring out of me. Instinctively, I knew He'd been waiting to see me. When I was closer, I felt like I was the most beloved and cherished person to Him.

I ran to Him, into His arms, pressing my face against His chest. Spiritual love flowed from Him into my spirit with quivering quickness as fast as lightning lights up a dark sky. Jesus was not a stranger. He knew me, and I knew Him. It felt like the last time He held me was only a moment ago. His love was all-encompassing, and I realized it was the only thing I needed.

If I could combine the love I experienced on Earth from before birth until the day I arrived here, it didn't compare to one second in His arms. Maybe if all the love I'd ever known could be collected and multiplied by infinity, it would come close. His very touch exuded love beyond measure. I was undone in every way. Then, a few words from His heart to mine put me back together. They were, 'you believed in Me.'

His voice was full of authority, and His words carried great weight. Every description of Jesus I learned about on Earth was a poor excuse to being in His presence. He was a warrior, stronger than anyone or anything the world had ever seen. He was a king, royal in every possible way. And He was my friend, my brother, and my father at the same time. He is the great love of my life, but I didn't know it until now. In His arms, I had never felt more alive or needed.

We sat back down on the rock, never losing our embrace. Water from his right sleeve was dripping onto me. It was hard to decide what gave me more energy, Him, or the water? Then I realized it was the same. He was the water, and the water was Him. Jesus is heaven, and heaven is Him. When I realized He was everything and everything was Him, I leaned back to look into His eyes. If someone's eyes could be every color, if someone's eyes could say thousands of words in seconds, and if eyes could be made of fire, it was His eyes.

"Jesus."

"Kessum, My beloved," Jesus said as though I were the only person that meant anything to Him.

My spirit felt as though it had been enlarged, filling beyond its capacity with happiness and joy. He knew my name; He called me beloved. Feelings of unworthiness bubbled up, but the second they tried to fill my thoughts, they were swept away by His love. Without speaking aloud, Jesus filled my heart with His admiration. His words replaced everything trying to enter my mind. The mistakes, the times I failed, and even the times I was mad at Him.

"Skipper was so happy to see you," Jesus said out loud, still holding me in His arms.

"I missed him. You know he's been gone for six years."

"To him, it was like he saw you yesterday. Your measure of time doesn't exist here."

"I can't believe I almost stopped believing in You," I said, looking into His piercing eyes.

"Are you sure about that, Kessum? You wouldn't be here if that were true."

Jesus relaxed His right arm while keeping the left one securely around me. He smelled like roses and sunshine, or how it smells in spring after a rain shower; it was familiar, like fresh mountain air. His love was like a warm, soft blanket surrounding me. It made me feel special, invincible, and powerful. He glowed with light, and with His arm around me, I glowed even brighter.

I looked toward the field, asking, "Why am I here?"

"This is your green pasture," Jesus told me.

My mind processed His words, then I slowly asked, "Can I, lay... down?"

Jesus stood up, taking my hand. We began running across the rich, lush green grass. He started laughing with childlike joy. Everything... for as far as I could see, joined in His joy. The grass didn't laugh, neither did the trees nor the water, but the rhythm, the music of this place, transformed from great peace to immense joy.

The green pasture morphed into a massive field of daffodils, and I could barely comprehend what was happening. As we ran through the flowers while holding hands, Jesus reached down and gathered an armful of brilliantly shining, golden-yellow daffodils. Smiling, He handed them to me as we continued gliding over the flowers. I held hundreds of daffodils in my right arm, my favorite flower. Light was glowing from every petal as I admired the gift Jesus gave. Closing my eyes, I leaned forward and took a deep breath of the fantastic aroma.

"My favorite flowers," I said aloud.

"I know, Kessum. I planted this field of daffodils just for you."

We continued soaring through the field of flowers, our feet never touching the ground. Jesus began to laugh, which made me laugh. We looked into each other's eyes, and at that exact moment, I knew this was where I belonged, not Earth. He turned His head, and I looked where He was looking. Up ahead, the flowers ended where the vibrant green grass began again.

The daffodils I held in my right arm close to my chest were pulsating with light. I smelled their delightful scent once more before releasing them. They flew in a semicircle, some just a few feet away, while others landed hundreds of feet away. The sounds they made as they went through the air reminded me of gentle fingers dancing up and down on piano keys. As each flower moved closer to the ground, it didn't fall like flowers on Earth do. Instead, its stem reattached itself to a stalk. Light shot up in tiny rays as the flowers rejoined the other daffodils. They moved gently, being blown by a soft wind.

Still holding hands, we left the field of flowers behind, entering a vast, plush field of green grass. There was nothing but grass as far as the eye could see. No hills, no valleys… until a question entered my mind. The question was because of the 23rd Psalm. If this is my green pasture, then where are the still waters?

When I turned my head toward Jesus, I could hear Him in my mind saying, 'Look again.' As we continued moving, I saw a beautiful lake with mountains in the distance. On the right-hand side was another field of flowers of many different shapes and colors. On the left side of the lake was a forest of beautiful green trees in various sizes and heights. Everything I could see was pulsating with sound, full of light and life.

As we approached the water, we began to slow down. I thought my feet would touch the ground, but they didn't. The magnificent body of water reflected mountains, flowers, and trees. It was like the most beautiful painting I had ever seen, some of God's most amazing work. Again, just within my mind, I decided I would never leave this place. It was mine. Jesus said it was mine. I knew I wanted to stay here forever and ever.

"I will always be with you," Jesus said, letting go of my hand, reclining in the grass.

It was perfect, the definition of peace. The grass moved gently with the never-ending rhythm of life pulsating softly. It was green, every shade of the color I'd ever seen, and at least a thousand more. Light rippled through the blades, then up and out into the atmosphere before becoming part of everything. If only I could keep this moment in every thought on Earth, I would remember there's no need to rush. I could take my time every day, remembering God and spending time with Him. Then, how angry I was at God before He brought me here entered my mind.

"I never left you, even when you were mad at Me," Jesus said.

Lying down beside Jesus, I reached for His hand. Everything I ever questioned about Jesus, the Father, or the Holy Spirit melted away. All I ever needed was the touch of His hand. All the things

I wanted so much on Earth were now meaningless. Now I knew without a doubt, all I ever needed was Jesus. What a tremendous waste of time, energy, and effort I expended on things that would not last.

The grass moved effortlessly beneath me. On Earth, that would have been very strange, but in heaven, it's normal. Light flowed through me and through everything around me. My thoughts came in rapid succession. Jesus is the light. I am His, and He is mine. Which makes me part of the light. The body that held my spirit, that I was in, wasn't me. Even though it wasn't me, I'm still me. That must mean I was full of the light even when I was back on Earth.

All the things my Aunt May tried to teach me as a child became crystal clear as I lay in the green pastures with Jesus. Now, I realize I barely understood anything she wanted to teach me. How many times did she tell me about God?

Aunt May would speak about heaven, but I didn't understand. My mind would drift when she started talking. It was random thoughts like, wonder what's for dinner, does Tommy like me, or why didn't Susan invite me to her party? Suddenly, I realized that's the way most people treat the things of God on Earth. They rarely stop and fully surrender themselves to spend time with Him. They become easily distracted by the mundane. When, by some rare coincidence, they hear scripture, their minds drift to other useless thoughts.

"They don't know what they're doing," Jesus answered me with a thought.

His magnificent voice flowed into my spirit. I had heard it before, on Earth, when I was praying. Now, come to think of it, there were a few times when I wasn't praying. So I thought about what He just said. It sounded so familiar.

"Yes, it's one of the scriptures people quote."

"Why don't they know what they're doing?"

"Because of the choices they've made. They have eyes that could be opened. They have ears that could hear. Within their body, I placed a heart that could be renewed. It's all about choice. Do you choose the world and everything that's in it? Or do you choose Me, leaving the desires for the things of the world behind?"

"I choose you!"

"You chose me here… in this place, but yesterday you denied me."

"If I denied you, how could I be here?"

"Because of the prayers others have prayed for you."

"I don't understand," I replied, turning to look at Him.

"There's a difference between believing and denying."

"I didn't mean to deny You. I'm sorry. I don't know why I make such stupid choices."

"You will have another opportunity to align your choice with truth because you can't stay, Kessum. There's still much for you to learn, to accomplish."

With a sudden sense of urgency, I stood up and looked around. The trees, grass, flowers, and crystal waters were so close, with tall mountains on the other side of the lake. I felt like this was my home; it had always been my home, and there was no way I would ever leave. Certainly not to go back to the dullness or chaos on Earth. Why would I want to do that when I could stay here and have peace forever?

"Because you have to go back and tell them who I am, tell them I'm coming back and they need to be ready," Jesus said, sitting up.

"Jesus, I don't want to go back. They are so mean to me; even the people who love me are mean," I begged, kneeling.

"Kessum, they don't understand that everything they do to hurt someone, they do it to Me. In the same manner, everything they do out of love for someone, they do it to me."

"How am I going to make them understand?"

"I chose you. You are stronger than you know."

"I will try."

"Always remember My words. *I was hungry and you gave me something to eat. I was thirsty and you gave me something to drink. I was a stranger and you invited me in. I needed clothes and you clothed me. I was sick and you looked after me. I was in prison and you came to visit me.*"

"Yes, Jesus," I replied, with tears filling my eyes as my heart burned with love.

"Remember, to tell them, Kessum, 'Whatever they do for one of the least of their brothers and sisters, they do it for me.' They will listen when you say My words."

His magnificent eyes pierced right into my soul. One moment, they appeared green, the next blue, and the next a color I'd never seen. I knew it was pointless to ask again, but I didn't want to go back, especially without Shane.

"Why would You choose me to come to heaven just to send me back?"

"You must fulfill your purpose."

"What's my purpose, Jesus?"

"Moment by moment, I will reveal My plans for your life. Listen to your heart, Kessum. Follow My Spirit." Jesus said, touching my chest with His finger of light.

Closing my eyes, I fell back onto the grass. In my spirit, I could feel Him healing me from so many disappointments in my life. The unkind words spoken by others and feelings of rejection simply faded away. Only His acceptance and the ability to embrace who Jesus made me to be remained.

I could see untold numbers of angels dressed in white surrounding me. Maybe I was back on Earth already. There was so much light, so much peace. Then there was Jesus, smiling as we glided again above a field of flowers. The angels followed close behind, singing a song of undying love for the King of Kings.

"It's time to go, I want to take you to My mountain," Jesus said.

We floated above the field, moving past the flowers, down the embankment to the water. The water changed from shades of blue to white and then green, all full of the light of heaven. The wind blew gentle waves toward the water's edge. Rays of light leaped up from the water, joining the atmosphere like vapor dissolving into thin air. The joy, the pure excitement, continually flowing through everything, suddenly became intense.

Jesus raised his right hand towards the water, and the wind began to slow. The waves ceased without Him speaking a word, and the water became perfectly still. When I saw His reflection on the water, my heart felt like it would burst. I was overjoyed. The definition of the word peace became abundantly clear. Jesus reached out to me. We slowly walked, hand in hand, onto the water.

The words in Matthew reverberated within my mind: *Oh ye of little faith.* What was happening? What was I experiencing? Did it mean I have great faith? The disciples of Jesus knew Him well. They traveled together. They learned many things as He taught because Jesus led by example. I was here walking, holding His hand, living water splashing gently around my feet, yet I barely knew Him.

When we reached the other side, the wind began to blow again. As we entered another beautiful green pasture, the waves started coming softly on shore. He took my hand, and we began gliding across the grass. Then, small rocks turned into boulders as we reached the mountain.

Looking up, I had never seen a mountain so tall. The color and texture of the rock seemed to change with height. It reminded me a little of the Grand Canyon. At the bottom where we stood, the mountain's colors were brown, yellow, and green. So many trees, bushes, and flowers grew from every crevice that I wondered where we would begin to climb. Then I noticed the animals. Birds, sheep, squirrels, and many other animals were active. They glowed, iridescent colors pulsating from their bodies. Light came from their feet, fur, eyes, and mouths. Every living thing, big or small, was so beautiful and more than alive.

Without explanation or warning, Jesus took my hand, and we ascended with incredible speed. For a few moments, I couldn't control my laughter. Jesus moved quickly, maneuvering up and around the mountain with great skill. It was more exciting than any amusement park rides I'd ever been on. It wasn't weird; it was supernatural.

Time didn't exist in heaven, but I remembered how passing time felt. What would have taken hours on Earth seemed like only seconds. Many things on Earth didn't exist in heaven, like mourning. For the first time in a long time, I felt no sense of loss or sadness when I thought about Shane.

Jesus and I stood on a large plateau with a 360-degree view. The mountain's colors and texture changed again. The brown rock bled into gray and white but still glowed with light. The white colored stone sparkled, reminding me of sunlight striking the ripples on Big Lake in Mississippi, looking like a million diamonds.

Without speaking, Jesus asked me to look and see. I turned to the left. I could not see what was below. Maybe whatever He wanted me to see was too far away. I turned to the right. There, in the distance, I could see a large city glowing with a brilliant golden light. A vast wall surrounded it, and I couldn't see the end. When I turned to look directly behind me, I could not completely comprehend what my eyes saw. It was like gazing into the Milky Way, that's, well, milky. It wasn't clear, but I could still see sparkling lights floating up, moving toward the city.

"This is only part of My Kingdom. When you return, I will show you more," He said aloud with authority and power.

"Is this Heaven?"

"Yes," Jesus answered, looking intently toward the city full of light.

"Is this the mountain of God people sing about?"

"Not how you're thinking, but yes, you could say that. I remember you singing one of those songs. It made Me happy," Jesus said, sitting down upon a well-worn rock.

"How did you hear me? I usually only sing when I'm alone."

Jesus turned to face me, fire in His eyes, "That's not true, daughter. You are never alone. I'm always with you."

"But what if we leave You?"

"You didn't leave Me. You didn't have Shane with you on Earth, and you were upset. You stopped talking to Me. So many souls… I've lost so many precious souls because of their lack of understanding."

"Help me understand."

"When trouble comes, they don't turn to Me. Sometimes, they even blame Me and turn away."

"I'm so sorry, Jesus. Now that I'm with You, I can feel how much I hurt You. I should have prayed. I should have turned to You."

"The Holy Spirit is ready to guide and comfort, but He will never interfere with your choices."

"It's hard to make the best choices when your heart is broken. I don't think I'll ever understand everything," I said, looking into the bluest eyes of pure love.

"Daughter, all things are in My hands. Still, I have an enemy seeking to destroy those I love."

"Why can't you protect us?"

"If you knew how often We shield you from harm, you would begin to understand your importance to the Kingdom of Heaven," He answered as a large colorful light-filled bird flew nearby.

"So humans are constantly in danger?"

"The battle is for the eternal soul. To cut short a life means the soul, the spirit, will not fulfill its purpose. Humans have an enemy who is the prince of their world. He wants you to blame Me for what he does."

"I still don't understand."

"Kessum, I came to give life in abundance. Death, loss, and destruction do not dwell in Me. If I controlled everything happening on Earth, could my enemy come to steal, kill, and destroy?"

"No, because You are full of love and righteousness."

"Just as My Father prepared a place for you, heaven, He prepared a place for Satan, hell, a place of everlasting fire. Lucifer and the angels who followed him seek to take all lost souls with them into hell."

"Wow," I said louder than I wanted, not realizing one word could change how the light around us moved.

He looked away in the direction of the city. "Life on Earth could be different. If people wanted more knowledge, more wisdom from the Kingdom of Heaven."

"Help me understand."

Jesus turned toward me, mercy in His eyes. "John 17:15 says, *I do not pray that You should take them out of the world, but that You should keep them from the evil one.* In the lives of believers and non-believers, something traumatic happens. For you, it was Shane dying in a car crash. They don't realize it's an attack from the enemy, who only comes to kill their faith, steal their dreams, and destroy their purpose and destiny. You see, somewhere in the plethora of lies circling the globe, they blame Me. They think, how could a good, loving God allow these things to happen?"

"Jesus, I never knew…"

"It's one of my enemies' craftiest weapons. He uses simple words to influence the hearts and minds of the world. Then whenever there's loss or destruction, death, or disease, even poverty… most people believe I'm to blame."

"I believed so many things about You that aren't true."

"I am the truth, the way, and the life, not death. There is no darkness found in Me. I do not want anyone to be destroyed. I want everyone to follow me, not even one to be lost."

"I know, but I still don't understand why Shane died."

Jesus looked into my eyes. "The day you asked, w*hy God*, it was Satan who answered you."

"I thought it was You, Jesus, but I knew it wasn't. Something inside my spirit told me it wasn't You, but I felt so lost."

"Many of My children don't even realize there's a war being waged against them. To defeat Satan, My people need to know the truth. I am the truth."

"I feel like I'm beginning to understand now."

Jesus looked away, saying, "If they really knew Me, they would never blame Me for what Satan does to them. He's the one who murders, robs, and crushes every human spirit he can. That is his character, and it speaks very loudly throughout the Earth."

"Why was I so blind? Why was I so deaf and dumb?"

"Kessum, you are wiser than you realize," Jesus said, reaching into the cleft of a rock, pulling out a flower.

It was red with pink and white dots, then pink with red and white dots, and then white with red and pink dots. As it swirled through the colors, light radiated in every direction. Jesus pushed back my hair, placing the magnificent flower behind my left ear. He whispered, "What can I give Him?"

I replied, "Give Him my heart."

"You were five, Kessum, when you memorized that poem and gave Me your heart. No matter where you've been or what you've gone through, I was there."

"Now that I'm here, I understand why I always felt like I was never alone. God is everywhere. I can feel the Father so strongly. He's in the flower, He's the grass, He's the mountain, and He's the song all of creation sings. I'm so overwhelmed by love right now. I feel like my spirit can't contain it."

"My Father is love, Kessum. We are filling you to overflowing while you're here. He wants me to show you something. Look," Jesus said, pointing down in front of us.

"It's so beautiful," I replied as Jesus held my hand.

"All that you see is heaven. To the north, to the south, to the east and west, everything belongs to My Father."

"You truly are the King of Kings. I'm beginning to understand what that means," I said, not letting go of His hand. Power was leaving His fingers, flowing into me. It felt like pure energy. I knew that if I stayed connected to the source of that energy, I would always be able to share it with others.

"Whatever belongs to My Father is mine. Everything you see, including you, is mine. You are more precious to Me than gold. You are one of the most beautiful things I've ever created. The day I formed you in your mother's womb, all heaven rejoiced. I was so proud the day you were born. All the angels in heaven were singing when you took your first breath. All heaven rejoiced again when you were five years old and gave me your heart. You have never disappointed me, never, not even once. I love you so much, Kessum, that I gave My life for you. Look into My eyes. You will see the reflection of the one I love dearly."

"I can't do it, Jesus," I said, falling to my knees.

"Not one of your tears was wasted. I collected every single one of them and put them in a bottle," Jesus replied, placing His hand on my head.

"Don't make me go back to that place. Please, please, please, I want to stay here in Heaven with You."

"There's a purpose for your life. You must fulfill it. No one except you can do it."

Jesus moved to sit down on the ground beside me. He put His arm around my shoulder as His love flooded my spirit. Deep inside, I still wanted to refuse, but feeling His love made it impossible. I would do anything He asked, no matter what I had to do.

My eyes were closed, His arm still around me, when I heard His voice inside my mind say, look up. We were no longer on the mountaintop but in a beautiful, lush green valley. In the distance, there were houses, some big, some huge. The roads looked like glass with light shining through them.

"Let's walk. I want to show you something I have for you."

"For me?"

"Yes, for you," Jesus answered with a smile.

This time, we walked, not hand in hand but side by side. The same music and energy came from everything: the grass, flowers, trees, birds, and even the road we walked on. The light emanated from everything, filling the very air with vitality. I took a deep breath, wanting to fill myself with this power. I knew I could accomplish anything if there were any way to go to Earth, full of this energy.

"What do you think?" Jesus asked, pointing down a narrow road.

"It looks like I'm back in Mississippi, except for the houses. They don't build houses this big back home. Goodness, it looks like twenty people could live in that country mansion."

"Twenty people could, but that's not its purpose. It's given to honor those who honored Me, My Father, and Holy Spirit."

After walking a little further toward the house, I began to see every flower native to South Mississippi, plus more. The flowers' scent was the most amazing thing I'd ever smelled.

"Wow! Whose flower garden?"

"It's for you," Jesus said, taking my hand, stopping at the end of a long walkway.

At the end of the path was a gorgeous home with an enormous front porch. On opposite ends were matching swings, six rocking chairs, and a love seat with two chairs. Beautiful plants and colorful flowers filled every space. Jasmine vines climbing up from the corner posts were in full bloom.

"I don't know what to say," I said, turning to hug Him. "It's the most beautiful house I've ever seen."

"Jesus pointed to a large Spanish Oak in the front yard. "This is your tree."

My eyes locked onto the tree, studying the branches, remembering the last time I saw it, and feeling a surge of emotion. "Jesus, this is so much."

"I was there when you climbed on its branches and were in awe at its beauty. You were just a little girl, but you understood the tree's value even though you were young. You begged your parents not to sell the house because of this tree."

"The woman who bought our house cut it down. I cried and cried when I saw that it was gone. I couldn't believe anyone would cut down a healthy tree that was that old. There was no reason for her to cut it down other than she didn't like having acorns and leaves in her yard."

"It's safe here. It will never be cut down again."

The urge to go and touch the trunk, to climb the branches, shot through me like a burst of energy. Some invisible force stopped me. It was as though I knew it wasn't the right time. It was the right place; it was my place, but I had to wait until I returned.

"Is there water, a pond or lake, with willow trees?"

"Yes, of course, there'll be water with willow trees and lots of flowers to love. You'll have so much to do when you return," He answered, once again putting His arm around my shoulder.

Somehow, I knew within my spirit that He was creating it the very moment I asked about the lake. Then, when I asked about the willow trees, their roots began to grow deeper as their long branches began to sway in the gentle wind.

Was it in the asking, or did Jesus give me what my heart desired? Standing at the end of the long walkway to my heavenly home, I couldn't see the lake or the willow trees. It was in my mind, or maybe my spirit, where I could see the long branches swaying near the water's edge.

The music that seemed to come from everywhere changed to a softer tempo. We stood staring toward the house for what seemed like a long time, but time can't be measured in heaven. The moment I turned to Jesus, I was overcome by a deep sense of peace.

My thoughts turned toward Mom and Dad. What would it be like for them if I died? If I never went back to Earth. I closed my eyes, and when I opened them, we were transported to another place.

Jesus stretched out His hand for mine. We walked up a winding trail towards a house that looked more like a castle than a house. Angels flew from all directions, some landing on the roof, others flying into the light. Everything felt instinctively familiar but foreign.

As we walked, Jesus spoke to me in my thoughts without opening His mouth. Memories from my childhood brought a flood of emotions. He gave me a chance to think as we walked the rest of the way to the front door.

Once inside, we walked down an extraordinarily long hallway with no pictures on the walls. Almost near the end, we went into a small room. It was empty except for two brown wooden chairs. The presence of God was so tangible, the atmosphere felt heavy. I sat down, looking at my hands. The feeling of being surrounded by angels went through me, but I couldn't see them.

Something important was about to happen, but I didn't know what it could be.

Then it began. In thin air, a review of my life, from childhood to teenage years and then adulthood, appeared before me. These events came from different years of my life, some sad, some happy.

It was how my decisions, words, and actions affected others that reverberated within me the most. The ripple effects of how my choices impacted people, most of whom I never met, were overwhelming. I would have been more cautious about what I said or did if I had known that every human interaction causes long-term consequences.

We left the room, walking up many flights of stairs. Jesus pointed to a door on the right. Reaching out, I turned the knob, entering a massive room similar to a library. It was filled with wooden bookshelves. Light shined everywhere without an obvious source. Big, white books sat on the shelves lining the walls. In the middle of the room was an extremely long wooden table. Sitting at the end of the table was one man. He looked up at me when I entered the room.

An invisible force pulled me toward the man sitting at the table. My spirit was drawn to His light. I had to speak with Him. I turned to tell Jesus I was going, but He gestured for me to go before I could say anything.

Who was this man sitting alone in this enormous room at an expansive table surrounded by huge books on extremely tall bookshelves? Why would Jesus leave me here to talk to Him by myself? As I approached, I realized there were only two chairs. He was sitting in one; the other was empty. I pulled it out and sat down.

Jesus looked like the average blue-collar 32-year-old man you might see in America. He wasn't overly handsome. However, his facial features were pleasant. He didn't wear a crown. He wore a simple white tunic with a gold sash tied at the waist.

In contrast, the man I sat down beside was handsome. He had brown, well-manicured hair that accentuated his striking face. His tan skin radiated health, and His tailored suit spoke of wealth. Even though everything about Him was impressive, His eyes captivated me most. They looked exactly like the eyes of Jesus, and His face radiated the same captivating light.

He never said anything, but I knew Him. His spirit and mine had always been intertwined. My breath, the very substance of God, which kept me alive, came from Him. We looked at each other, communicating silently. The peace surrounding Him gave me everything I needed to face returning to my life.

Without speaking a word, He asked me to close my eyes. The instant both lids touched, I was in another place, seeing things I'd only heard about or seen in movies. Flames of fire lit up desperate faces as they screamed in horror. The sound was different from the screaming voices of people arguing. This type of screaming, of wailing, only comes from extreme pain. Everything I could see was in darkness, except for the sparse light from the flames.

The air was almost entirely void of oxygen. Gasping for every tiny breath, I wondered how anyone survived. It smelled of sulfur and rotting flesh and was worse than anything I'd ever smelled. The heat was intense, worse than any summer day or bonfire I'd experienced.

Demons of every shape and size ran, walked, or crawled, doing horrible things to people. The demons laughed when people cried out in pain. They screeched with excitement when people screamed in agony. The grotesque creatures celebrated, yelping like dogs when anyone cursed God. If anyone dared to cry out the name of Jesus, they whimpered as if it hurt them. Then the demons tortured the soul who said Jesus even more severely.

Along the sides of the enormous pit stood metal cages. They reminded me of jail cells, except for one thing. These cages didn't have doors, and none of them had a roof. Instead, each person being tortured in a cell was bound in a particular way. Some had chains on their hands, feet, or both. People were chained up in peculiar positions, some with their arms above their heads and some hanging upside down. Others had been tied down on a table or in strange-looking chairs. Each cell contained more than one demon doing unspeakable horrors to young and old people. How their bodies could be maimed and mutilated to such a great degree and not die made me feel almost overwhelmed with fear.

Finally, when I didn't think I could watch what was happening for another moment, it was over. Standing to my feet, I fell to my knees, crying, "Oh please, God, please, I never want to go there. I never want to see that again. Tell me what I need to do to be with You! I'll do anything..."

"Kessum, hell is not your final destination. You were allowed to see, that's all. I'm asking you to warn others, people on Earth you know, and even strangers."

"Why? Why did I have to see that?"

The handsome man reached out for my hand. The moment our hands touched, I knew who He was, I felt calm, and I knew the answers.

When I sat back down, He pushed a book toward me. It was the biggest book I'd ever seen. The edge of the cover was white. It was open, and I looked down.

"Look what is written," He said, pointing to the right-hand side.

She will author a book during her lifetime. We will send help and provide everything she needs to accomplish this task. In this book, she will describe heaven and hell, recounting what she has witnessed. It will be published and translated into different languages. Around the world, people will read this book and be drawn into the Kingdom of God. The book will be entitled...

"Why did the words disappear, Holy Spirit?"

He pulled the book back towards Himself, closing it, replying, "Some things aren't meant to be known. When it's the right time, you will know what to name the book."

"I don't know how to write a book; I struggled in high school, even writing book reports. Is that really what You want me to do?"

"This is your book, Kessum. Writing about heaven and hell is one of many things you will do," He said, picking up the book, putting it in my hands.

"Oh my goodness, it's heavy."

"It's the book of your life." He smiled, reaching over to take the book out of my hands. He sat it on His right side, then turned toward me.

"Why is it so thick? How long will I live? I don't want to be away from You that long."

"You will be satisfied with a long life, but always remember I am with you. I will teach, guide, and comfort you until your return."

"Every plan I had for my life was taken from me when Shane died. I don't even want to go back," I said, looking at the enormous book again and contemplating how many decisions I would have to make.

"I will help you with every decision when you ask Me."

"How will You help me? I'll be... who knows, a billion miles away. Facing the world alone, no husband or family of my own."

"Look at me," He said, taking my hand.

Energy and peace enveloped me like a baby held in its mother's arms. I realized the Holy Spirit had always been with me. There had never been even one day He wasn't there. He was there in the good times. He was there when things went wrong. I had never been alone. I would never be alone. Never.

"Help me now. Help me carry this feeling, this understanding, back to earth. Now that I've experienced it, since I've been here, I won't survive going back without it."

"Look at me," Holy Spirit said, taking my other hand, "I have everything you need. You will never lack anything. I – have – everything – you – need."

"Sitting here with You, I know that's true, but what will happen when I return?"

Suddenly, great joy overtook my spirit, and I laughed, knowing I could never contain it. Then joy invaded my thoughts, filling them with saving grace and mercy, and I began making unrealistic plans. If I could reach out to touch every person on earth, I felt they would be irrevocably changed. There would be no hate, no wars, no killings, no sorrow, and no pain. It felt like I was so full of the Holy Spirit, like a mighty river flowing out of my innermost being. If I could carry this back to Earth, I could do everything He asked me to do. My thoughts were spinning with possibilities until Holy Spirit began to speak.

"You will write a book, and I will be with you, always. The book you will write will help many people. Don't be afraid to tell the truth; never get upset if anyone disagrees with your story. Remember the ripple effects of your decisions. Never be quick to anger, keeping yourself from being offended as much as possible."

"I will do my best. I'll write the book. I won't care what people think or say about me."

"It's even more important to love, but you already know that Kessum. Be blessed, my beloved; know I'm your Advocate. I will always be with you."

The door opened. I wouldn't have noticed except for the Holy Spirit looking away from me, down the extraordinarily long table. Two tall angels dressed in white came through the door, stopping just inside. They were there for me, but I didn't want to leave. I had so many questions. I felt like Holy Spirit held all the answers.

"I'm closer than you think. When you return, and have times when you wonder where I am. I'm right there," He said, touching my chest.

His fingers released wisdom into my spirit. All the questions faded away. Now, they instantly became unimportant. There was an inner sense of knowing that everything would be all right. No matter what happened or how my circumstances changed, I would be all right.

"If I could write about how You made me feel, and people could feel it for themselves, that would be enough. It could put an end to so much worry and anxiety. People would feel this amazing peace and have much more hope."

"You will write about it; many will read your words. Those words will give some comfort; some will experience peace and some hope, still others will doubt and ridicule every word," the Holy Spirit said, standing up.

When He stood, the light in the room moved in waves. Even the books from floor to ceiling emanated light in ripples. I heard the music again, which I hadn't realized was in the room. I sensed that the music, the light coming from everywhere, from everything, was like air. Invisible to the eye, but you can hear it and actually feel it. The music was like God the Father, everywhere and in everything.

Holy Spirit opened His arms, wrapping me inside them, whispering, "He's everywhere, and yes, He is everything."

"Thank you," I said, lingering in His arms.

"When you're ready, they will show you the way."

The walk back beside the long table to the angels gave me a chance to look at some of the books. It made me think about the many lives, stories, and decisions held within the pages. Without God providing Jesus as our savior and the Holy Spirit to guide and comfort us, it was easy to see how people could stray. It became apparent how so many lives were affected by poor choices.

Even though I was tempted to look back, I didn't. It would have been harder to leave. The angels ushered me out without touching me. I began to wonder how old they were. Neither one looked older than twenty-five in human years. Then I thought, I don't think angels in heaven age. They both had masculine features, one with blonde hair and the other with red. They also wore long, white tunics, but the red-headed one had a green sash, and the other a brown sash. I didn't know if different color sashes meant something, but I knew I didn't need to know the answer.

We walked down the stairs, never exchanging words. I followed the Angel with red hair while the one with blonde hair followed me. I felt safe with them, even though nothing could harm me in heaven. The angels, like everything else, shimmered and glowed with light.

The instant the red-haired Angel touched the doorknob of the mansion, we were in a different place. We were in an area filled with rolling hills. Lush, beautiful green grass moved softly, blown by a gentle wind. There were other angels, and they were dressed in a white tunic. All were dressed identically except for the color of their sashes.

Walking up and over several grassy hills, more and more angels joined us. They were strikingly different in every way possible.

Masculine and feminine, tall and taller, fair-complexioned and dark, but everyone was magnificent. Some angels spoke a language I did not understand, while others spoke English.

He was there, standing atop a hill in the distance. As we approached Jesus, the angels' excitement and the light coming from their clothes and bodies grew. The underlying music became louder. The grass beneath our feet grew longer, and more light rose from each blade.

The closer we came to Jesus, the more joy seemed to overtake everything and everyone until it felt like an eruption of overwhelming joy was imminent. It reminded me of a kid at a Christmas parade. As you looked up the street, you knew the floats were coming. Then, you could hear sirens and other people's excitement in the distance. You could walk past the crowd and see the floats coming down the street. It felt like anticipation and excitement of what you might see and receive.

Climbing up the last hill, I was suddenly climbing alone. I didn't want to take my eyes off Jesus, but I couldn't help myself. I turned around to see the crowd of angels, some kneeling and some bowed in worship. As they began to sing, I thought this was the most beautiful sight I'd ever seen.

I would have fallen to my knees if He had not called my name. When I looked, he was waving, beckoning me to come to Him. I walked, then ran as fast as I could.

He opened His arms, and I almost jumped into them. We turned round and round, laughing with great joy. His embrace was like nothing I'd ever felt before. The love of Jesus was completely pure. It was all-consuming and all-encompassing. If I could write a thousand books to describe it, it wouldn't be enough. There aren't enough human words to even come close.

"I want to show you something," He said, putting His arm around my shoulder.

We walked down the hill and back up the next one. In the distance, stood a sea of people—so many people were watching us. The sounds of heaven continued, and the light glowed brightly from the vast crowd. I knew they were God's people, even though it was hard to see their faces. I wondered if my grandparents or Aunt May were in the crowd.

Jesus knew my thoughts and pointed to the left. I knew in an instant it was her, my Aunt May. She appeared to be about 30 years old; her hair was long, brown, not short, and grey. She wasn't wearing glasses, but her smile was just as warm as I remembered. I wanted to walk to her, but I knew I couldn't go, so I waved. She waved back, then blew a kiss.

"Thank you for letting me see Aunt May. I've missed her so much," I said, searching the crowd for familiar faces.

"What you are seeing is your future and some of your past. This gathering of souls will be touched by your life, by your choices. You will remember this and the impact of following Me and the Holy Spirit guiding you. Look at how your choices will affect you and others. Can you count them, Kessum?"

"No, Lord, I can't. How will my life affect this many people?"

"Just by being who I made you to be. In the book, you will write everything. You will tell everyone about Me, about heaven. You must also write about what you saw in Hell."

"I'll do my best, Jesus. Will I remember everything when I go back?"

"No, but you will remember what you need to remember."

"What if I'm still mad at You? I want to be a Christian, but…"

"It's easier than you think to follow Me."

Gazing across the sea of people, I wanted to draw closer to God because I needed to learn His ways and do what He asked. If Jesus said it's easy, then I need to believe Him.

"I can do it. I will follow You," I replied, falling to my knees.

When I did, everyone in the crowd got down on their knees. Then I could hear the sound of voices in the music. Maybe it had been there the whole time. I don't know. Now the voices grew louder, and the words I was hearing, I'd heard before in a song.

"Holy, holy, holy is the Lord God Almighty, who was and is and is to come," Angels sang.

The voices, barely above a whisper, created an energy. It came from the field full of thankful souls, into my soul, standing on a grassy green hill. The energy pulsated throughout my entire being, giving me courage and strength.

Everything in heaven was foreign but familiar. There was this immense understanding and a decisive knowingness—a knowledge that God was everywhere, even in me. He is our creator. I am His creation. On my knees, bowing before Jesus, it was the closest I'd ever felt to Him, and I wanted to stay forever.

When I finally raised my head, the sea of people was no longer in front of me. Instead, I was kneeling at the feet of Jesus. He was sitting on His throne. The light emanating from within Him, which I thought couldn't be any brighter, was even more brilliant. The song the Angels were singing earlier was easier for me to hear now. So, with everything that was within me, I joined them.

"Holy, holy, holy, is the Lord God Almighty. Who was and is and is to come!"

The sense of God being near kept me on my knees, face down. For a moment, I would look up at Jesus. His face shone intensely with luminous light radiating around Him. It was bright and so overwhelmingly beautiful that I could only look for a moment before closing my eyes.

In my mind, I heard a voice saying it was time to go and see, but I ignored it while singing a song of love with the Angels. Again, I heard a voice saying it was time to go, but I didn't want to go. I wanted to stay and worship Jesus forever.

In a flash of light, the voices of the Angels faded until it was barely a whisper. The same humming, the soft music I heard before, was back. That's when I realized it was the pulse of heaven. The very heartbeat, the life of heaven, was the beautiful sound of music. Everything, the trees, water, flowers… even the air, e-v-e-r-y-t-h-i-n-g worshipped all the time. Still on my knees with eyes closed, I wondered if it was the same on Earth and I'd never noticed.

"No, it's not the same," Jesus said, knowing my thoughts.

I looked up, realizing we were back near the beautiful field by the crystal-clear water. Skipper slept in the grass. Jesus sat on the rock near the water's edge. Behind Him, a large willow tree had grown. Its long green branches blowing in the wind, with light gleaming from every leaf, were almost too beautiful to comprehend.

"Skip, come here, boy, come on, boy, come here, Skipper."

Skipper woke up and began running, jumping up on me with damp paws, and licking my hand. His fur was soft beneath my fingers. Skipper seemed younger here than when he passed. I searched nearby for a stick. He always loved playing fetch, but I didn't see any. Jesus pointed away from the river to my left side. Only a few feet away was the only stick on the ground, and it was just the right size for playing fetch.

"Here, boy," I said, holding up the stick.

He jumped with anticipation, and I threw it as hard as possible. He ran, gliding above the grass like Jesus and I had earlier. With the stick in his mouth, he ran right back to me. After I petted him, he set the stick at my feet. I reached down to pick it up and threw it again. Skipper ran to retrieve it, but he didn't return. Instead, he ran straight ahead, disappearing into the thickness of the daffodils.

"You will see him again," Jesus said.

Sitting down on the rock beside Him, I said, "Thank you. I've had other dogs, but there was always something special about Skip."

"I know."

"Jesus, do I have a choice to stay with You?"

"Kessum, for you, there is no choice. You must return."

"Can I accomplish what you've asked me to do?"

"Yes, you will receive a Crown of Glory, My faithful daughter. People will be drawn to Me through your words. You will have as many readers as there are stars in the night sky. I will be your inspiration. Holy Spirit will be your guide. My Father will give you strength."

"I'm not sure what to tell them."

"Kessum, tell them the truth. Tell them that the road to heaven is less traveled than the road to hell. Many only want the things of the world, things they can see, touch, feel, and taste. You can't see, touch, or taste the Holy Spirit, but you can feel Him. When the Holy Spirit is around you or within you, you can feel Him. You cannot see the wind, but you can feel its strength. The same can be said of Holy Spirit. You cannot see or touch Him, but when you receive the infilling of the Holy Spirit, you can feel Him within you. Then, every breath you take, every thought you make can be filled with grace."

"What do I say about hell?"

"Kessum, tell them what the Holy Spirit showed you. Also, I will give you a story to share. On Earth, humanity builds two towers. One is plain, with a cross at its top. On this tower, there is a simple sign. 'Giving away free directions to heaven this Sunday.' Inside, a few souls kneel at the altar, praying. The collection plate is passed around to help the needy and poor. The other tower is painted red and black. It's covered with flashing lights. Inside, there is no room; the crowd is shoulder-to-shoulder. There's gambling, alcohol, singers, dancers, drugs, and around-the-clock partying. They throw away their money on machines, gambling tables, sports scoreboard outcomes, and anything that gives their flesh a moment's pleasure. When these people leave this tower of sin, they are broke and hungry. They go to the tower with the cross because they give food to the poor and needy. Once their bellies are full, they do whatever it takes to return to the tower of sin. They could stay at the other tower, giving their money to help someone in need, but they don't. Their interest is not in heaven or where they'll spend eternity; they are only interested in what they can have today."

"Yes, I will tell them the story of two towers, but I still have many questions."

"Ask me whatever you want," Jesus said, leaning down and picking up a shiny rock.

"Will I remember any of this when I get back home, I mean, back to Earth?"

"What's important... you will remember. The rest will be given as you live... day by day. We will always give you what you need."

"What was the purpose of Shane's death? We had our whole lives ahead of us. We had plans."

"Kessum, do you know I have a plan for your life?"

"But Jesus, I don't understand why Shane, the love of my life, died so tragically. How can that be part of Your plan?"

"It wasn't," Jesus replied, tossing the rock in the water.

I watched the rock skimming across the water's surface, and then the water rose, covering the rock with light. The rock was inside the light, and the light was inside the rock. The sight brought back a memory. It was a parable I heard in church, 'Don't build your house on shifting sand, build it on The Rock.' I thought about Jesus' words. I said, "Help me understand."

"My plan is for you to have an abundant life, overflowing with love, peace, and joy. That is My plan for you and everyone who follows Me. My enemy also has a plan for your life, to end your life. He wants to take everyone and everything you love and utterly obliterate your joy and peace. Do you understand?"

"Yes, but Shane believed in You. He went to church. He was a good person."

"There's something you haven't understood yet. I am King of Kings. Satan is only a ruler of the Earth. Do you remember reading the scriptures that tell the story of him taking Me up to the top of a mountain, showing Me all the world's kingdoms?"

"Yes, I remember. It was after You fasted for 40 days?"

"Yes, that's when he tempted Me. He said he would give Me everything I could see if I bowed down and worshiped him. Kessum, how could he give Me what wasn't his to give?"

"So it was Satan. He killed Shane?"

"Satan stole his life but not his eternal soul. With Shane's death, Satan is attempting to destroy many lives, stealing your faith in Me, turning your joy into mourning, and robbing all of you from fulfilling your purposes."

I turned to my right, looked into Jesus's face, and asked, "How do we fulfill our purpose when it hurts so bad?"

Jesus touched my chin with His hand while staring into my eyes. "Kessum, keep your eyes on Me, don't look to the left, don't look to the right. No matter what, you keep your eyes on Me and do everything with My Kingdom on your mind."

"Jesus, I will keep my heart, soul, and mind on You and Your Kingdom."

"Kessum, for you, that will be simple. You have seen me. For others who haven't seen me, it will be hard."

"Maybe it will be easier when I tell them about heaven."

"To know any of My children are struggling… think about your dad, Richard. How does he feel when you have difficulties? Then what if he had already solved the problem but you didn't want to know how to do it? In the same way, and even greater than a human, I've given everyone on Earth the opportunity to receive the keys to the kingdom. All they need to do is seek and they will find them."

"Some of us don't even know that there are any keys. Aunt May served You with all her heart. If she had known about the keys or understood how to use them, the end of her life would have been different."

Jesus reached out, raising His left hand, saying, "The keys are in The Word. I am The Word. Every mystery of life and life more abundant is revealed through Me."

"It's so easy to understand what You're telling me here. What's going to happen when I'm back there? Will I remember what You told me?"

"You will remember what you need to know. Some people read The Word and grow in mercy and love. Others who read the scriptures are filled with doubt and anger."

"Her husband, Uncle Joseph, was that way. He was mean; he didn't even want Aunt May to attend church. He didn't want her to go anywhere; he just wanted her at home. He died suddenly one night of a heart attack. One day, he was here, complaining and being a bully to everyone, and the next day, he was gone. I don't understand why he had to be like that. Aunt May loved him so much."

"Kessum, sometimes Satan allows people to have a life free of pain and suffering. He doesn't want them to turn to me. What they don't understand is that they are being controlled. They aren't making their own choices. The truth is that these souls are in a prison because of their choices. Satan leaves the door open for a season, giving the illusion that they are free to leave. Then the door closes, and he locks the lock. It's too late."

"So, are the prison cells on Earth?"

"You are not understanding. This type of prison holds human spirits that are eternal, not meant to be contained. It cannot be seen with human eyes."

"It's like when someone is a prisoner of drugs or alcohol. They can't live free. It's a prison, but there aren't steel bars holding them or someone forcing them to stay in addiction."

"Kessum, think of the house I built for you."

"Yes, with my favorite tree in the yard and that huge front porch?"

"Yes, that one. I have prepared a place for you and many others. Satan is also preparing a place for many. My place is filled with life, beauty, and love. His is full of misery, pain, and darkness."

"Will I forget what the Holy Spirit let me see in Hell?"

"No, but in time, it will fade. Don't wait to write it down."

"Now that I'm here, everything on Earth, everything in my life seems incredibly small and insignificant."

"No, you are more important than you understand. Every person born has a purpose to fulfill. You are feeling the immense vastness of the spiritual world. Your physical world is like a drop of water in a large ocean. It's the same water, but it's only one drop."

"If the spiritual world is so vast, why can't I feel it?"

"Because you don't pray. You listen to other people pray. You ask people to pray for you but rarely talk to Me personally."

"I don't know how to pray. Nobody ever taught me."

"Everyone prays differently; just talk to Me like you would a friend. Pray to Me every day like you love Me and want to spend time with Me. Always remember, there's power in prayer."

It was the first moment I looked away. My mind was full and racing with thoughts and feelings I'd never felt. I needed to make plans to accomplish my purpose. I was ready to get to work, to get things done. I was not afraid of the challenges or obstacles. Then it hit me.

"I don't want to fall in love again, Jesus. What if he dies or gets sick? I can't lose someone else I love."

"Nothing is ever lost. Come, I want to show you something," He said, standing up, stretching out His hand.

We walked in silence along the water's edge. The rhythm of heaven, the low musical hum, slowed as the sound of the crystal-clear water moving downstream mixed with the melody. The flourishing, abundant life of everything had a vibration, rich with purity that could not be matched on Earth. Everything seemed to be in perfect order. There was not one blade of grass out of place. All of heaven looked and felt harmonious.

This time, we didn't run. We strolled around each bend of the river's path. He wasn't holding my hand, but He walked close beside me. The same sensation, the same knowing that God was everywhere, made me feel loved and protected.

My mind was clear of questions. I was content, sharing this sacred space, walking beside Jesus in the most beautiful place I had ever seen. Trees planted beside the water, leaves blowing gently in the wind of heaven. Every color of grass on Earth and so many more felt like an expensive carpet under my bare feet. Bushes covered with flowers, growing by themselves or together, grew everywhere I looked.

Then I saw the horses—two white horses walking toward us. One was a little bigger and taller than the other, but both were magnificent. We walked to meet them in the field of green grass.

"It's time to ride," Jesus said, helping me onto the horse's back.

"Where are we going?" I asked, sliding forward, grabbing the horse's mane.

"You don't have to hold on so tightly; you won't fall."

"I've only been on a horse once in my life. It wasn't this big."

"Trust me and your horse. She won't run too fast, and she'd never let you fall," Jesus said, getting on His horse.

"Okay, if you say it, I believe You," I answered, adjusting myself and loosening my grip.

He circled me twice, saying, "I have something I want you to see."

With those words, we were off. The horses ran across the green grass into the field of daffodils. The light came from every-thing- the grass, flowers, and horses. It rose from the ground like tiny rays of bright sunshine. Then I noticed I didn't have the same clothes on. I was dressed in a long white linen dress. My arms looked healthier and stronger, and my body felt firm, not so skinny. I reached up to touch my hair. Before, it was thin and could barely grow to my shoulders. Now it was full and longer than it had ever been on Earth.

There was an exuberance in my horses' gallop that wasn't there when we left the crystal river. At first, I thought it was because of me. Then, I noticed a young woman with blond hair riding toward us. She also rode on a white horse, dressed in a long white dress. Jesus slowed down to be right beside me. He pointed in her direction, and I noticed a much younger child riding with her, a little brown-haired boy.

The question ran through my mind. Who are they? But I didn't have to ask. I knew they were my children. I knew that I knew I had nothing to worry about or any reason to be concerned. All I had to do was live and follow Jesus. If I kept my heart pure and my eyes on Jesus, one day, I would hold them in my arms.

We turned back toward the river, and my children turned in the other direction. It was brief and from a distance but I was thankful. They were beautiful, strong, and healthy. As we rode back, I wondered why I couldn't meet them. Why would He let me see them but not speak to them?

Our horses slowed to a trot, and Jesus laughed loudly. "You don't have to understand everything, My daughter; just believe, have faith!"

"I will have faith, I promise," I replied, pushing down questions bubbling up in my spirit.

"I have a question for you, Kessum," Jesus said, both of our horses stopping near the water's edge.

"What is it?" I asked, looking right into His fiery eyes.

"Do you love me?"

"Yes, I love you."

"Do what I ask you to do."

Before I could answer, I felt myself slipping off the horse, across the heavens, falling, just falling, and falling until I stopped. The pain woke me. Screaming for help, I heard an old familiar voice. It was my voice. I was back. I was suffering. I was in my very broken body, missing Jesus and already longing for heaven.

CHAPTER TEN

"It's time to call it."

"Man, she's so young. One more time."

"I don't think there's enough juice, but go for it," the EMT said, looking at his watch.

"Come on, lady, don't give up," he said, moving the paddles closer.

"It's 9:23…"

"Wait, I've got a pulse."

"Hang in there, Kessum, we'll be at the hospital soon."

The EMTs worked on my body, doing what they could to help. I was barely conscious, occasionally hearing voices or feeling their touch. Shock took over my senses, so I didn't feel the full impact of the pain. Instead, I felt unearthly, almost like I wasn't here. When I opened my eyes, all I could see was fog. When I tried to speak, there was no sound.

"Female, 21, fell down a staircase, head trauma, left and right arm injuries..."

The voices trailed off as I felt myself begin to move. When I opened my eyes again, I saw a woman. Her voice was soft, but I couldn't understand what she was saying. Other people were moving around in the brightly lit room, but I didn't know them.

When I closed my eyes, I could still see heaven. I could still see Jesus. I drifted back into my memories of heaven. There were so many questions, and I still had so much I wanted to ask Jesus.

Why didn't I ask Him if one second on Earth was like a day, an hour, or a week in heaven? Will we need anything, or is everything provided? Can we go swimming or skiing? Do they have restaurants, churches, and schools? Are there bathrooms, and do we take showers? Will we have cars, trucks, trains, or planes? I don't remember seeing any. Will we have jobs? Do they eat pizza or hamburgers in heaven? Do we celebrate birthdays? Do we sleep in heaven? Do we dream? I still have so many unanswered questions.

Then, in my mind, I began praying, asking Jesus if I could come back to heaven. Then I promised Him if He'd let me come back, I wouldn't ask any questions. I just wanted to see Him again and hear His voice.

"Jesus, please let me come back!"

"We're losing her," a voice said.

My mind had little connection with my body. I could see that I was in the emergency room. I heard people asking questions and giving commands. The next moment, I was floating, weightless, like in a dream. Then I began having flashbacks of heaven. Memory after memory of things I saw when I was there flooded my thoughts.

"You need to stay awake, Kessum," a voice said, close to my ear.

"The surgeon will be here any minute," a woman said. She touched my arm, and I could sense her concern.

"Ow, that hurt!"

"She's still with us. Just a few minutes, Kessum, and it won't hurt," she replied.

That was the moment I became aware of the pain. At first, it was my right forearm, throbbing with each heartbeat. Then, my head ached with every beat. It felt like someone punched me in my lower back right before I drifted off to sleep.

When I woke up in the ICU, the nurse called for my parents. Then I saw Mom and Dad standing on either side of the bed, looking down at me. As I drifted in and out of consciousness, they looked blurry, and their words didn't make sense.

The next day, the doctor came in and stood at the foot of the bed, looking at a clipboard. My head felt heavy, and I couldn't raise it to see him fully. He handed the clipboard to the nurse and walked to the side of the bed.

"How's my patient?"

"She's been better," the nurse replied.

"Well, it looks like you've had yourself a nasty little fall. We've managed to patch you up, and it'll take a little time to heal. But you've got time, Ms. Howards, plenty of time."

"What happened?" I managed to ask.

"You don't remember? Your neighbor said you were in a hurry to get to work. Then, one wrong step. Man, sometimes we don't know what a day can bring. Luckily for you, he called 911 and got those EMTs to you fast. They got that ticker of yours restarted, which saved your life, young lady."

"Then it was real…" I whispered through swollen lips.

"Yes, very real indeed."

"I don't remember."

"There's time to remember; I don't suggest it. Sometimes, it's better to forget certain details. How is your pain level?"

"Now that I'm awake, about a ten. What's wrong with my left arm?"

"You've got some torn ligaments in a couple of places. Your right arm has two fractures, one upper and one lower. Your right wrist is broken, along with your left ankle."

The doctor turned, looked back, and motioned for someone. The door opened wider; he whispered to a woman, then told me, "The nurse will increase your medication. You should only be in the ICU for a couple more days, then we'll move you into a room."

"Have you seen the angels?"

"What angels?" He asked, looking up at the nurse on the other side of the bed.

"The ones that keep coming in and out of this room."

"Nope, no angels here. Have you seen any angels?" He asked the nurse with a chuckle.

She inserted a needle into my IV, smiled, and answered, "No, I haven't seen any angels. What do they look like?"

"They're all different, just like humans. That tall one is one of the angels I saw in heaven. He's here to protect me."

The nurse and doctor looked in the direction of the angel. They turned back with blank expressions. Without another word, the doctor turned and walked out. The nurse patted my hand. My eyes closed, and once again, the dreams began.

In my dream, I was back in heaven with Jesus. We were together, walking down the light-filled road. Jesus glowed with light and love greater than any I'd experienced on Earth. It came flowing from Him, surrounding me, flooding my spirit. His eyes like fire penetrated my soul as He watched me looking at the beautiful home He had prepared for me. Everything within me wanted to run up that road, dash up those steps, and sit on that big porch. I understood why I couldn't go. It wasn't my time. It would be my time one day, and I knew I would be there forever. We would often gather there, enjoying ourselves. No one would ever be in a rush to leave; we would want to be together and feel content and happy. No one would hate each other or want to be somewhere else. No one would gossip about anyone behind their back. Not one negative thing would cross their minds or lips. It seemed so distant now, but I could barely wait for that day.

A voice interrupted the dream, saying, "She's not awake yet, Richard."

"Dad," I whispered.

"Hey, sweetheart. How are you feeling today?"

"Why would you ask her that?"

"It's okay, Mom."

"We brought flowers, but the nurse said we needed to keep them until they move you to a room," Dad said, leaning over to look at me.

"Your dad took the flowers back to the car. Let's hope the heat doesn't wilt them." Mom said, pulling the sheet to my neck, tucking it under my side.

The pain of her hand pushing the sheet under my back caused me to move, which created even more pain. She gently pulled the sheet out, then pulled it down, away from my neck. The look on her face when she saw tears streaming down my cheeks made me want to stop crying, but I couldn't.

"It's going to be okay, Kessum. We will take care of you. You don't have to worry."

"Dad. I can't do this. I don't want…"

Mom leaned forward, saying, "We just thank God you're here. I'm sorry I hurt you. Next time, I'll ask before I…"

"I can't even get out of bed."

"Don't worry about that right now. In no time, you'll be on your feet. So many people are praying for you," Dad said, wiping my tears away.

Mom took a tissue, wiping tears from the other side of my face, and said, "You are such a strong girl. Everything is going to be okay; you'll see."

There was a quick knock at the door, then I heard a familiar voice ask, "How's our patient doing?"

"She's a little upset right now, Doctor."

"That's completely understandable. She is probably late for a two-week vacation to Hawaii, and now she has to reschedule," he chuckled.

Mom didn't laugh. Instead, she asked, "What's wrong with her back?"

"Well, Mrs. Howards, your daughter has swelling in the lower back. There may be a couple of compressed discs, but let's hope that's not the case. We'll redo the tests in a few more days and see what they look like. In the meantime, we are still treating her for a concussion. She took a couple of bad knocks."

Dad turned away, lowered his voice, asking, "What about her heart?"

"Kessum's heart is completely healthy. Every test we ran shows no issues whatsoever."

"Then why did that happen?" Dad asked, walking around the foot of the bed, standing beside Mom.

"Sometimes there's simply no explanation for what happens in the human body. Science is great. Medicine is fantastic. I make my living from both, but neither one is perfect. I'm sorry. I have no idea why her heart stopped. Maybe from the trauma? Maybe from the concussion? I can only give you my theory."

Their voices trailed off as I sought relief from the pain by closing my eyes. As I floated off into a drug-induced sleep, Dad's question kept going through my mind. 'What about her heart?' Then a voice, sweet as honey, purer than fresh white snow, spoke within me. 'If not your heart, then what, My love?'

It was finally moving day, and everyone buzzed around, getting things in order. Since the day of my accident, I have had no appetite. Now, I crave everything: hamburgers, pizza, steak, baked potatoes, pancakes, cookies, ice cream with whipped cream, and cherries.

Dad said he would get me anything I wanted, but Mom stopped him. She told him I needed to eat whatever the hospital brought me. Of course, she was right, so Dad decided we would have a going-home party with any food I wanted instead.

The following day, there came a knock at the door. The nurse looked at me and I nodded. She told them to come in. I was surprised to see Linda with her husband, Jordan.

"Kessum," Linda said, making my name seem longer than it is. "How are you? We've been praying for you ever since we heard the news."

"I'm so much better. I went to heaven and met Jesus."

"We heard about that," Jordan said, holding a big bouquet.

"Let's put these right over here," the nurse said, taking the flowers and putting them on a table. "We may need to bring you another table, Ms. Kessum, just for your flowers and plants."

Linda looked around the room, saying, "My goodness, there are so many. If we had known, we could have brought something else."

"No, I love flowers. Thank you," I replied, trying to sit up to see them better.

Linda moved quickly, grabbing the edge of the pillow. The nurse moved to the head of the bed, pressing something with her foot to raise it. The pain of moving was intense, but I tried not to show it. Jordan sat down in a chair, turning his attention to the television.

"We can turn it up if you want to watch something," I offered.

"No, that's okay. I know Linda has a lot to tell you. I hope you know how blessed you are, young lady. God is watching out for you."

"Yes, He is watching over me and you, too, Jordan. He is amazing and loves us more than we can understand."

"Will you hand me a tissue?" Linda asked the nurse.

"Here's the box."

Linda pulled one out, folded it in half, then wiped tears from my face, asking, "You got to meet Him?"

"Yes, I did. All those times you told me about Him, but I didn't get it. Before this happened, I almost didn't believe Jesus was real. After Shane died, my faith was gone. I was so angry at God."

Linda looked over at Jordan as the nurse walked out of the room. Jordan walked to stand beside my bed and said, "We want to pray for you. Is that okay?"

"Yes."

They held my hands and reached across the foot of the bed to join hands. Jordan closed his eyes, and Linda followed. I watched as they both prayed silently, their lips barely moving, before Jordan began to speak.

"Our Father in heaven, we come to You with our friend, Kessum, who You placed on our hearts. We ask that You heal her body, Lord; heal her spirit. We are thankful for her, this beautiful person You put in our lives. Please bless her greatly, all the days of her life."

The atmosphere in the room shifted. I closed my eyes, sensing the angels of God nearby. Goosebumps covered my body as Linda gently squeezed my hand. Then a gentle wind blew from my left side. It was barely enough wind to move my hair and I wondered if they felt it, too. My heart began beating a little faster as I felt a tingle moving from the top of my head to my toes.

Linda cleared her throat, praying, "You are the Alpha and Omega, the beginning, and the end. You decide when we are born and when we die. Lord, you are the Bright and Morning Star, and we worship You. We thank You for Kessum. You are a great God, and You do great things. Please heal her, bless her, Lord. Bless her indeed, in Jesus' name, amen."

Jordan pulled two tissues from the box. He handed one to Linda and gave the other to me. He looked into my eyes before turning to sit back in the chair. Linda wiped her face, took the tissue from my hand, and wiped away my tears.

"Linda, Jesus broke every chain of bondage off me when I was in Heaven. I'm completely and utterly free!"

"That's amazing! Tell me more," she pleaded, with her voice breaking.

"Do you know God has given us the power to choose? Whether we make decisions for good or evil is completely up to us. The effects of our choices ripple like waves through generations, affecting many souls, known or unknown. I believe that's one of the reasons Jesus taught us how to pray and gave us examples of how to do it. We communicate with God, asking Him for His will to be done. His will is always for good; He's full of mercy. It is our enemy that's full of evil and strife. Still, God gave man dominion over the Earth. He also gave us free will. He's given us the ability to choose."

"Kessum, how did you learn this?" Linda said, eyes wide and voice high-pitched.

"When I went to heaven," I answered, hearing a knock at the door.

"Come in," Jordan said.

"Hey, I hope I'm not disturbing anything. I'm Kessum's neighbor, Chance, Chance Actman," he spoke softly, extending his hand to Jordan.

"No, not at all. Come in; nice to meet you. This is my wife, Linda."

"Hey, Chance, I'm glad we finally have the opportunity to meet you." Linda walked around the bed and took his hand, pulling him closer into a hug. "Kessum and I were just talking about heaven."

"That's not a subject I've studied before, but since Kessum's accident, I will say it's been on my mind."

"We aren't the most educated on the subject either, but we want to learn more," Linda replied, walking over to stand beside Jordan.

"I want to study it also, but who has time? With two boys, a job, and a wife, life gets a little busy," Jordan said, clearing his throat.

"One of those subjects needs to be hell."

"You're right, Kessum," Linda said quickly. "It's something more Christians should learn about."

"That's a subject I don't want to know more about, much less talk about. I'm sticking with the positive, not the negative," Jordan said, nodding.

Linda walked back to the side of the bed, taking my hand. "Goodness, how did we get into such a heavy conversation? I'm sorry, Kessum. We just wanted to stop by and hopefully make you feel better."

"Talking about heaven and hell makes me feel better. That's what Jesus asked me to do."

Linda squeezed my hand, saying, "I know it is, sweetie. Look, you get some rest. Next time I come, I'll bring you something good to eat. Then we'll talk about anything you want."

Jordan stood up, reached out his hand to Chance, saying, "Hey, it sure was nice to meet you. Thanks for taking care of Kessum. You're a good neighbor."

"I just happened to be at the right place, at the right time. I didn't do anything special."

Linda took Jordan's hand, led him toward the door, and said, "Chance, it's good to meet you. Kessum, we are just a phone call away. Let me know if I can do anything for you."

"Thanks, Linda. I'll see you soon."

Jordan walked out the door while Linda said, "Yes, I'll be back, maybe tomorrow, but if not tomorrow, the next day."

"Okay, thanks again for the flowers."

"They are a nice couple. How do you know them?" Chance asked.

"I met them when I went to church with my future mother-in-law. Well, she's my ex-future mother-in-law. Linda stayed in touch with me after my fiancé died."

"I'm so sorry. I had no idea," Chance said, looking around the room.

"It's one of those things you don't tell a stranger."

"Yes, that's true. We are strangers, in a sense, but not so much now. At least not to me."

"You saved my life, didn't you?"

He set a small wooden box just out of reach on my bed, taking a few steps back before saying, "No, I most certainly did not save your life. I stayed with you, beside you, until the ambulance came."

"Thank you for that. It must have been hard."

"Hard?"

"To see it. See me like that, watch me die."

"It wasn't easy. Well, that's an understatement and completely inappropriate. Yes, it was hard, and I have been genuinely concerned about your well-being. Since I'm not family, they wouldn't let me visit in the ICU."

"I'm okay, just broken in a few places. The worst one is my head."

"You know a concussion is considered a traumatic brain injury, a mild one, but still serious. It will affect your brain function, and you may experience memory loss among other symptoms."

"Are you studying to become a doctor?"

"Oh no, I'm in school to become an engineer, specializing in aerospace. I'm enthralled by every single aspect of anything that flies. Airplanes, helicopters, space shuttles, rockets, even birds fascinate me."

"I can tell. I've never heard you get this excited," I said, looking at his face. His brown eyes sparkled with enthusiasm. He pushed fingers through his thick brown hair, moving it off his face. I'd never looked at him, or maybe it was the angle, the lighting. Chance was handsome, not an Adonis, but handsome in his own way. His skin was perfect, with no blemishes, and his body looked healthy.

"You haven't heard my voice enough to analyze my emotions. However, I am excited about this subject. Also, I feel a sense of relief after seeing you."

"Chance, can I ask you a question?"

"Sure."

"Do you believe in Jesus?"

"Jesus... of Nazareth?"

"Umm, yes, that's the one. Are you a Christian?"

"I was not raised to be Christian, but I have studied Christianity a few times since I was eleven. Something about it always intrigued me."

"When I died, I went to heaven. I met Jesus when I was there. I miss Him so much."

"Confusion is one of the effects of concussion," Chance replied, picking up the box.

"I'm not the least bit confused. Jesus is as real as you and me. He's more real than you and me. Heaven is more real than this place. Earth is so unreal compared to heaven. I didn't want to come back."

When someone knocked on the door, Chance said, "Come in."

Two men walked in, and the tallest one said, "Ms. Howards, we're here to take you down for your CT scan."

"I'm going to get out of the way," Chance said, moving closer to the bed.

He stared down for several moments while the men silently waited. He didn't say anything. When he picked up the box, he smiled. Sitting it on the side table, he reached down, squeezed my hand, then turned to walk away without saying goodbye.

"Are you coming back?"

He stood at the door, looking back over his shoulder. He shook his head from side to side, then answered, "You don't know me, but there's nothing that would keep me from it."

It seemed he had said no with his head and then yes with his words, which made me wonder how I should respond. As I looked at him, he reminded me of Clark Kent, the character in the old Superman movies. He looked a little nerdy, but underneath it, he was strong.

"Good, we'll continue our discussion."

"I'd like that," he said, nodding before walking out.

Two days later, after multiple visits from Mom and Dad, Linda and her boys, Seth and Brett, Cooley, and even Arthur and Annie, I still hadn't seen Chance. Lately, each time there was a knock at the door, I expected it to be him. It made me wonder if I said something to offend him.

It didn't bother me if my questions about Jesus or heaven made people uncomfortable. I asked everyone, even my doctor, if he believed in Jesus. I asked them if they were Christians. If they would talk, I spoke about heaven and, sometimes, the things I saw in hell.

When Chance walked in with Tommy and Sarah, I was surprised. We lost touch, partially due to distance and partially because I was still mourning. The last chance I had to talk with Tommy and Sarah was a few months after Shane's funeral. Tommy had a job in New Orleans, and they moved just outside the city to Metairie.

"Sarah," I stammered, smiling, trying to lift my hand.

"Oh my goodness, Kessum," she said, rushing over and leaning down, touching her cheek against mine. "How are you doing?"

"I've been better," I said, looking at Tommy and Chance.

"I told you I'd be back." Chance sounded nervous but looked happy. He touched my foot, then stepped back, looking around the room.

"How'd you meet this character?" Tommy asked, patting Chance on the back.

"He's my neighbor who called for help when I took my spill."

"So he's your hero, not your zero," Tommy laughed, putting his arm around Chance's shoulder.

"Do you know each other?" I asked, wondering why Tommy was teasing him.

Sarah touched my hand, saying, "These guys go way back, all the way to diapers. Tommy's mom is Chance's dad's sister. They're cousins."

"Yes, now I see the resemblance. It's in the eyes and their noses," I said, trying to scoot up. Pain caused me to moan, which made all three of them step closer.

"Goodness, Kessum. I'm sorry we didn't get here sooner. I didn't know how bad…"

"I'm going to be okay, Sarah. Will you move the pillow? Chance, will you help me? Take my left arm."

"Is that better?" Chance asked, wrapping his arm around my shoulder, gently pulling me forward while Sarah repositioned the pillows.

"Yes, thank you."

Chance and Tommy sat down, watching television while Sarah and I talked. She told me about her family, Tommy's family, and some of our old friends. She also told me they had a date for their wedding. They planned to send the invitations soon. The ceremony was scheduled at the Arbor Room at Popp Fountain in City Park in the heart of New Orleans. They loved living in Louisiana and couldn't imagine starting their lives anywhere else.

Sarah insisted that I stay with them as soon as I was out of the hospital. We would shop in the French Quarter and have fresh beignets with hot chocolate at Café Du Monde. We'd picnic at New Orleans City Park and ride the trolley around the city. Then we would have to go to Jackson Square and see the Saint Louis Cathedral.

The one person she didn't bring up was Shane. In one way, she probably didn't want to upset me. In another way, by not even mentioning his name, she did.

Tommy and Sarah stayed for a bit longer, which made me happy. Even though I felt horrible and probably looked worse, they acted as if everything was normal, which was a good diversion from my current reality.

When they decided to leave, we all said goodbye. I thought Chance was going, too, but he closed the door behind them. Then he turned to look at me, staring at me with sparkling brown eyes.

"You look like you're ready for a nap. I should come back later."

"No, please stay. I'm a little tired, but I've been waiting to see you."

"I didn't know the appropriate time to wait between visits. I researched it, but there isn't clear information. That's when I calculated the longest suggested time with the shortest and decided to come today."

"I'm glad you did."

"Today seemed like the most appropriate decision, considering your injuries."

"Alright, I'm glad you figured it out. But for future reference, you can visit anytime you want. I'm not going anywhere anytime soon."

"Is this a reference to your life in general or the time you will be required to stay in the hospital?"

"I think a little bit of both," I answered, shifting uncomfortably in pain.

He rushed back to my side, his eyes asking what he could do. I lifted my left hand, and he took it. With his right arm around my back, we shifted my body, relieving some pressure on my lower back.

"You are in so much pain. Why don't they give you something that will help?"

"They are, but I've asked them to give me less. I don't like feeling so out of it all the time."

"Kessum, what will you do after you leave the hospital?"

"I'm going to do what Jesus asked me to do. It's the only thing I need to do before going back to heaven."

"I meant with your apartment. It's on the second floor. You won't be able to walk up and down the steps. I could ask the manager about getting you a ground-floor apartment."

"I haven't even thought about where I would go. I guess I'll go back home with my parents."

"Richard and Pam said the same thing. It is the most logical scenario in your situation, but I want you to know that if you decide to stay in your apartment, I will help you."

"Thank you. That is so kind of you to offer."

He looked at me, almost smiled, then asked, "Did you open my gift?"

"Yes, I'm sorry. I forgot to say thank you."

"Poetry is good for the mind."

His eyes looked toward the window as if looking far into the distance. His voice changed from serious to dreamy, and his body relaxed. There must be something about poetry that helped him with the uneasiness I usually felt when we were together.

"Will you read one to me?"

"Sure, let's see," Chance said, reaching for the box.

"Read me your favorite," I said, watching him thumb through the pages.

"So many favorites. Aw... here is the one I want to read today."

"I Wandered Lonely as a Cloud" by William Wordsworth

I wandered lonely as a cloud
That floats on high o'er vales and hills,
When all at once I saw a crowd,
A host, of golden daffodils;
Beside the lake, beneath the trees,
Fluttering and dancing in the breeze.

Continuous as the stars that shine
And twinkle on the milky way,
They stretched in never-ending line
Along the margin of a bay:
Ten thousand saw I at a glance,
Tossing their heads in sprightly dance.

The waves beside them danced; but they
Out-did the sparkling waves in glee:
A poet could not but be gay,
In such a jocund company:
I gazed—and gazed—but little thought
What wealth the show to me had brought:

For oft, when on my couch I lie
In vacant or in pensive mood,
They flash upon that inward eye
Which is the bliss of solitude
And then my heart with pleasure fills,
And dances with the daffodils."

"Daffodils…"

"Are you okay, Kessum?"

"He picked daffodils for me."

"Who?"

"Jesus gave them to me when I was in heaven."

"You know, I have been studying heaven the past few days and what happens to the human brain when it's starved of oxygen."

"Chance, you can say whatever you want. It happened. I died. I went to heaven. I met Jesus. He told me to tell people about Him, and I will do that."

He moved slowly, opening the box to put the book of poetry inside. Then he sat down in the chair. Looking toward the window, he said, "Kessum, let's just say I don't believe in Jesus or that there's really a place called heaven. How would you convince me that heaven is real?"

"I shouldn't have to convince you. If you know anything about me, you know I'm not a liar. Besides that, believing in Jesus is a choice. It's called faith."

CHAPTER ELEVEN

One year. Three hundred sixty-five days since I'd fallen down that flight of stairs. Time after time, I revisited that morning in my mind. Why didn't I slow down? Why didn't I leave the phone behind? Would being a few minutes late for work have mattered in the big scheme of things? The unanswerable questions and the possible answers changed absolutely nothing.

It's one of those strange things about the past. You consider ways you might have changed it, maybe by turning right instead of left or slowing down instead of being in a hurry. No matter how much thought you put into what happened, it happened, and nothing will change the outcome. There is only one good thing about reliving the past. It provides the ability to change the future, the here and now, this very moment by using knowledge and wisdom.

Since that fateful day of my accident, I learned many lessons. One of the most valuable was to slow down and not be in such a hurry. The other was to really live my life. I realized that if I wanted to live life more fully, then my view of the world had to change.

The American dream was no longer the rudder of my ship. If college worked for me, great, and if it didn't, great. I realized that my former priorities in life were no longer important. The big house, the fine car, and the expensive vacations didn't look the same. Instead, my heart longed for the things of God. Every chance I had to talk about Jesus, God, or Holy Spirit, I took it, and I thanked God every day for my life.

When I first came home from the hospital, Mom and Dad didn't want to hear about heaven. They both believed my memories were just dreams, none of them real. Unfortunately for them, they were a collective audience for my testimony. It didn't take long before both of them had become more interested. Now, they were telling everyone about heaven and hell, even asking strangers if they could pray together for their salvation.

On the first anniversary of my near-death experience, Mom and Dad insisted on celebrating. They insisted on honoring the day God gave me back to them. I didn't really want a party, or them to make a big deal over it. At the same time, I loved my parents, and I honored them by saying yes to a party.

People were going in and out, or around the side of the house all day. Men set up a big white tent, then carried chairs and tables to the backyard. Women brought food into the kitchen and began preparing to serve dinner. Other women and men brought everything needed to decorate and make it a beautiful night.

The dress Mom and I had bought for the occasion was one of the most beautiful dresses I'd ever worn. It was long, falling midway below the knee. It was white cotton with tiny yellow flowers. When I put it on, it just felt right and made me feel good.

"It's time, sweetheart," Dad said, knocking at the door.

"Be there in a minute," I replied, studying my reflection in the mirror.

"Don't take too long. Everybody is waiting," he said, tapping the door again.

"Dad," I said, opening the door, catching him in the hallway. "Is he here?"

"No, not yet, but I'm sure he's coming."

"I'm not so sure about that."

"Kessum, this celebration is for you, for your life. If he's here, that's great; if not, don't let it bother you."

"Okay, Dad. It's just that he was there when the accident happened. I want him to be here tonight. It doesn't matter if we don't have the same beliefs. I wish it didn't matter to him either."

"Look, all we can do is pray that God intervenes in his life. I would have given up on him long ago if it had been up to me. Sometimes, Chance is the nicest guy you'd want to meet, and other times, he can be as stubborn as a mule."

"Hello, Richard."

"Chance, we were just talking about you, wondering if you'd make it tonight," Dad mumbled, walking back to the living room.

"It's good to see you, Kessum. You look beautiful," Chance said, his eyes moving from the floor to my head and back down again.

"Thanks. I'm glad you're here."

"You are even more beautiful than my memories. How long has it been?"

"Just a few months. How are your classes going?"

He looked behind him as voices drifted from the living room. "Everything is going okay. I've missed seeing you and..."

"Me too. Do you want to…"

"Yes, if you don't mind going with a stubborn ole mule."

"How can you keep a straight face when you say that?"

"It's one of my superpowers," he replied, extending his arm.

My hand slipped between his arm and chest. His cologne wafted through the air of my childhood bedroom. It was exactly how I remembered it: masculine, earthy, with an undertone of sandalwood. As I rested my hand on his forearm, he flexed his muscle. The tension between us rippled like gentle, invisible waves as we walked toward the living room.

Dad pointed at the back door and then rushed to open it for us. Eyes from every direction watched as we walked through the door. Some people were well-known, some were acquaintances, and others were unknown. Chance patted my hand with his other hand, briefly smiling before pulling his shoulders back as we walked out to the party.

In the backyard stood a white tent adorned with at least 1,000 twinkling white lights. Flowers in yellow, white, and purple sat in large vases in the center of the tables. Beautiful music played softly as we walked down the stone path.

Trina emerged from the crowd, her long blonde hair bouncing as she rushed toward us. "Kessum, you look so beautiful."

"I'm so happy to see you," I replied, letting go of Chance's arm and wrapping my arms around my friend.

"I wouldn't have missed it for anything. Charleston isn't that far," she replied, turning to take my hand.

"Who's here?"

"Everybody who's anybody. Tommy and Sarah," she said, pointing to the left. "Cooley is somewhere over there. Oh, and there's Kelsy and her sister, Tammy."

"I thought Tammy didn't like me," I whispered.

"Well, she does now," Trina laughed, then whispered, "Are you ready for this?'

"Yes, I'm ready."

We reached the edge of the tent; Chance walked to Linda and Jordan's table. Trina let go of my hand, motioning for her dad to come over.

"Kessum, how are you, beautiful?" He asked, hugging me closely, not letting go.

I leaned into his embrace, replying, "I'm doing better, Mr. Watson. Thank you for coming."

"Wouldn't have missed it for the world. I needed to check up on my old buddy, Richard. He's been keeping a low profile lately."

"That's probably my fault. I've been keeping him busy."

"I'm glad to see you doing better. Sorry, I haven't been around in the past few months. I've been going up to Tupelo almost every weekend."

"Dad's new girlfriend has him doing the long-distance thing. I already told Darrin there's no way I'm doing that," Trina said, searching the crowd for her boyfriend.

"You better give me a hug, girl," Cooley said, walking toward me and Trina with his arms stretched out wide.

Trina wrapped her arm around his waist and said, "Everybody from here to New Orleans can hear you, Cooley."

He hugged me so hard. For a few moments, I wondered if he would let me go. I stepped back, watching Trina wave at her boyfriend, then walk away before asking, "Where's Tammy?"

"She didn't come. She wasn't ready on time, so here I am."

"Hey, no big deal. I'm glad you're here. It would have meant a lot to Shane for you to be here tonight."

"Man, you talk about missing somebody. I wish he were here, but then you wouldn't be having this party."

"Have you talked to his parents yet?" I asked, looking in their direction.

"Yeah, I saw them. I tried to talk to Tyler, but he's changed a lot. That kid used to talk my head off. He had more to say than any other kid I'd ever met, but tonight he barely said anything to me."

"Maybe it's because of what he's been through, or maybe he's just growing up," I replied, looking for Tyler.

"Hey, I wanted to ask you about that guy, Chance. Are you two dating or something?"

"It's something, but I'm not sure what. We mainly have fun, and then we don't talk for a while, then we have more fun."

"He sounds like an idiot to me," Cooley said, staring at Chance.

"Hi, Kessum. Sorry, I didn't mean to interrupt," Linda said, reaching for my hand.

"No, we were just catching up. Have you ever met my friend, Cooley?"

"I don't believe I have, but maybe somewhere along the line, we've crossed paths. I'm Linda. Nice to meet you." Linda extended her hand to Cooley.

Their voices blended with the other voices and music. My eyes drifted from one side of the tent to the other. Several guests were engaged in conversation at each table. The night had only begun a few minutes ago, and people were still arriving.

The vases on each table, full of flowers, carried me back. Every time I saw a daffodil, I was back in that field. Jesus was holding my hand as we glided, as we ran. Jesus leaned down, filling His arm with the biggest bouquet I'd ever seen. But it was the smell that never left my mind. Since my return, I've smelled every daffodil I could. Nothing even comes close to what I remember. Everything on Earth, including flowers, paled in comparison to what I experienced in heaven.

My mind drifted deeper into the memories. Only now had I begun to grasp the tremendous gift Jesus had given me. If it hadn't been for Jesus and the Holy Spirit, if They had only shown me heaven, and not hell, the burning desire to tell people would probably stop. Then I could live my life how I wanted and not be compelled to tell everyone what happened to me a year ago.

When I closed my eyes at night, all I could see in my mind was Jesus. When I slept, I dreamed of the Holy Spirit and that enormous table we sat at with my book. When I woke up, trying to go about my daily life, I could feel God in everything; He's everywhere. It had become impossible for me to be the person I was before the accident. It was also impossible to stay quiet because of what I'd seen and experienced.

"Darling, do you need to sit down? Do you want something to drink?"

"I'm okay, Mom."

"You were somewhere else, sweetheart," Dad said, taking me by the arm.

With Mom on the left and Dad on my right, we walked to our table in the middle of the white tent. A teenage girl came over with a glass pitcher. She poured water into our glasses, then whispered something to Dad. The water reminded me of the crystal river where I first saw Jesus. As the cool water passed my lips, I closed my eyes. In my mind, He was still there, sitting on the rock with His hand in the water. When I thought of the water, the lines from scripture played in my mind. '*He who believes in Me, as the Scripture has said, from his innermost being will flow rivers of living water.*'

Suddenly, my eyes opened wide. It hit me like a ton of bricks. Jesus is the living water. He is the crystal river I saw in heaven. That river is in me because I'm in Him, and He is in me. That means everywhere I go, the living river, the living water, flows. Jesus comes into my heart and goes out to others through me.

"Are you feeling okay? You've got that deer stuck in headlights look."

"I'm better than okay, Mom. It's been a year since I fell down a flight of stairs. It's been a whole year since that day when I was in such a rush because I was afraid to be three minutes late for work. A year of talking, thinking, and trying to sort out what happened to me. Was it real? Did I die? Did I go to heaven? Everybody has an opinion, but in the end, what really matters? Did it happen to you? Did it happen to them? No, it happened to me. Say what you want, but I've never been a liar. I'm an honest person."

"Look, there's no reason to get upset. You don't have to defend yourself. We're all here to celebrate your life," Chance said, kneeling beside me.

"I know, and that's exactly what I want to do. Is it time to eat, Dad? I'm starving. What about you, Chance?"

"I'm ready to eat. What about you, Pam?" Chance asked, tapping Mom on the arm.

"Yes, I'll let the caterers know it's time to serve dinner. It's your favorite, Kessum, lasagna with cheesy-garlic bread."

Chance joined us, sitting across from me. Dad prayed over the food and party guests. Mom and I said a few words, thanking everyone for being with us and praying for me. Peace filled the tent, and all I wanted was to worship Him. Instead, a plate of food was set before me and everyone else sitting at a table. There was only one way this kind of tranquility overtook the backyard. Angels had to be nearby, ready to do God's will.

Some of the guests had little spiritual sensitivity and began to eat. Others knew something special was happening, so they closed their eyes or quietly prayed. The food was not more important than this moment. What other people's thoughts or opinions of them were not more important than God's. They needed to be in His presence the same way I do. We are the peculiar people spoken about in the Bible. We don't give excuses or explanations about our behavior to people who would never understand. It wasn't always easy living in a world that doesn't pursue the supernatural things of God. But after what happened to me a year ago, it was all I knew, and it was all I wanted.

CHAPTER TWELVE

We sat across from each other in the back. I sat on the bench, and he took the chair. The Greenhouse always made me feel better. In a way, it had that feeling of home, and I wondered why, since it was nothing like home. The inside was small and could only seat a dozen or so people. Maybe it was the food. It was always made fresh by people who care about what they serve. But then again, perhaps it was the decor and the array of local art. Regardless of all of these things, who can resist a cute café on the downtown streets of Biloxi?

Chance ordered a special biscuit plate with a bag of Zapp's Potato Chips. For me, it was the quiche of the day, made with steak, asparagus, and parmesan. When the waitress brought our food, Chance stared at me, waiting to see if I would pray. Instead of taking his hand, I bowed and prayed silently, blessing our food.

Always the gentleman, Chance waited until I picked up my fork before he picked up his biscuit. His manners were one of the things I liked about him. He also had a way of putting me at ease. The months after my accident, he helped me a lot. Day after day, he would come by my parents' house after work, helping us with whatever we needed. On the weekends, he stayed with us, sleeping on a cot in the hallway near my room, so my parents could sleep through the night.

"Why so quiet?"

"I'm just eating. I was hungry," he answered, biting into a chip with a loud crunch.

"Me too. I skipped breakfast."

"I didn't skip breakfast. It was at 5:30, before I went to the gym."

"I forgot you switched gyms. Do you like it?" I asked, looking toward the door at a lady walking into the cafe.

"Not too much. I'm thinking about switching back."

His dark hair was longer than usual. His skin glowed with the evidence of recent days in the sun. After swallowing, I said, "I'm sure they'd be happy to have you back."

"At fifty dollars a month, I'm sure they would," he replied, getting up, walking to the garbage can.

"You ate so fast."

"Take your time," he said, reaching across the table, putting his hand over mine.

"I'm almost full."

"Just eat what you want. They just took cookies out of the oven," Chance said, before getting up.

He walked away, and all I could think about was why. Why did he ask me to meet him? It had been months since we last saw each other at my one-year celebration. Things between us were good at the party, but still, I wondered what was on his mind.

"Here you go, my lady. Thumbprint cookies, still warm, fresh out of the oven," he said, setting the plate down in the middle of the small table.

"They look delicious, but I'm only going to have one."

He laughed, "You say that, but wait until you taste it."

"Oh my goodness, so good. Maybe I'll take one for later," I said, taking another bite with a wily grin and laugh.

"You should. Kessum, you're probably wondering why I asked to see you. It's simple, it's because I've missed you. I'm sorry about what happened between us. I was so stupid and careless. Can you forgive me?"

"Yes, I've already forgiven you, Chance. God's love in me doesn't let me hold a grudge," I said, putting the rest of my cookie back on my plate.

"I don't blame you for being upset. I should have told you where we were going. I'm sorry it's taken me so long to apologize. I kept picking up the phone to call."

"Why didn't you?"

"I don't know. Pride, I guess. Every day, it bothered me. I knew I needed to make things right, no matter what happens between us."

"You took me to a meeting for atheists, telling me it was about investing in property," I said, standing up.

"Please," he said, reaching for my hand.

"What do you want from me, Chance?"

"I want you," he said, staring into my eyes.

"You know I care about you, Chance. This isn't fair."

"Please sit back down," he said, looking around. "Nobody is in here but us. Let's talk about it."

Sitting across from him, I noticed something I hadn't seen before. His eyes were sad, and he looked tired. I wanted to excuse myself and leave, but something in my heart made me stay, so I sat back down.

"What are we going to talk about? You have your life, and I have mine. It's taken me a long time since you left to figure things out. Without my faith in God, I don't know where I'd be right now."

"Jesus is your first love, I know that…"

"No, Chance, Jesus is not my first love. That's because I didn't know Him well enough when I was younger. Now I do, and I'm completely in love with Him. He comes first in my life. You're right if that's what you mean by He's my first love."

"I'm already upsetting you. Let's start over like we've never met before. Hi, I'm Chance Actman," he said, extending his hand.

"It's too late. We're too far down this road."

"I need you in my life, Kessum. I know I've never said it before, and this may not be the right place or time, but I want to say those three words to you. Give me a chance."

"Is this because I said I love you and you didn't say it back? Because I'm fine with that. I'm okay, really," I said, looking into his eyes.

"No, it's because I haven't found anyone like you. I want to see where this goes," he answered, moving the cookies so he could hold my hand.

"It'll never work, Chance. You are an atheist. I'm a Christian. I died and went to heaven. Jesus Christ is my savior. I'll always be a Christian."

"I know who you are, and that's why I'm begging you to let me be a part of your life," he said, squeezing my hand.

"Have you gone to church? Have you read the Bible since we had that 'discussion'?"

"No, I haven't gone to church. I don't feel comfortable walking into one of those places," he replied, letting go of my hand and sitting back.

"Are you still a member of the Great Southern Humanist Society?"

"I haven't been going to the meetings lately."

"That's not what I asked. Look, I'm not trying to change you. It is completely your choice to be an atheist. Honestly, if I had not been shown hell when I was in heaven, I wouldn't bother having this conversation with you."

"What do you want, Kessum? You want me to be in the closet or hide my beliefs like most people who don't believe in God?"

"No, I don't want you to be in the closet, but I also don't want you trying to change my beliefs. Nothing you say or do would persuade me to stop loving Jesus."

"I guess you don't want me to do what you're doing to me," he said, leaning back again.

"Look at your hand, Chance. See your fingertips. Every single fingerprint on every human that's ever been alive on this planet is unique to their fingers. Even that one fact screams to the normal person that there is a God."

"Then why is the largest growing 'religious demographic' in the United States atheists? We make up over 25% of the population. There are over 230 organized communities through-out the U.S."

"Sounds like you've done your research. Have you opened the Bible I gave you?"

"Yes, and some of it is ridiculous. I mean, really? Giants, witches, and a grown man being swallowed by a whale. And the guy with the ark, putting two of every creature on it. It would take a boat the size of Texas to hold all those animals and their food. I'm all for the morality it teaches, but some of those stories are total fiction."

"There's not one word in the Bible that's fiction, Chance."

"How can you believe all that stuff, Kessum?

"It's called faith."

"I have faith but not in religion. The only thing religion has ever done is divide people and start wars."

"That's not true. Who is it, when disaster strikes, that comes to help the helpless? Is it the government? Is it the atheist, the satanist? No, it's the people of God. They are the ones who clean up after tornadoes. They bring water and supplies to people affected by tragedies. They give of their skills, money, and time. They literally become the hands and feet of God, freely giving His love to everyone in need. You know it's the truth."

"Considering that only about a third of the world's popu-lation is Christian, I imagined people of all types would go and help disaster victims."

"Chance, there isn't any reason to raise your voice."

He leaned forward, smiled, saying, "You're right. I don't even know why we're talking about this."

"Because you don't believe in God."

While smirking, he shifted in his seat. "Can you blame me? Take a look around. If there were an *omnipresent* God that loves us so much, why would He allow such horrible things to happen?"

"Chance, we have dominion over the Earth. God gave us control from the beginning. We also have free will to do whatever we want. We choose for ourselves. God doesn't constrain us from choosing what is right or wrong. If you would just read the Bible, you could understand why our world is in its current state. So much of what man does displeases God. If you had only spent one minute in heaven, you'd know the way things are here is not how our Father wants them to be."

"I think you're confusing what happens when you die with your hopes for an afterlife. Scientists have proven that the near-death experience is merely a spike in cerebral electrical activity and multiple hormones being released all at once into the bloodstream. From what I've researched, you were experiencing hallucinations caused by the trauma of falling down a flight of stairs."

"I'm not confused, Chance. I think you are researching the wrong subject. The evidence for God's existence has progressed as science has progressed. They can't deny how carefully designed the natural world is, or the purpose of the universe, or how it all fits together."

"Perhaps that is a subject I'm lacking in," he said, looking toward the door.

"Before scientists began learning about these things, God said in Jeremiah, '*But I, the Lord, have a covenant with day and night, and I have made the laws that control the earth and sky.*' Chance, do you know that thirty laws of physics govern the universe? Each law isn't related to the other. However, each one is fine-tuned to make life possible. As an atheist, how do you explain that?"

"We don't. A wise man, Francis Crick, an atheist, said something to the effect of 'a man full of knowledge could only assume that the origins of life, the very first moment, must have been a miracle.' I bet you thought I believed in the Big Bang theory," he stated, smiling and nodding.

"Isn't that a contradiction in beliefs? Miracles are from God, not something atheists believe in."

Chance sat up straight, looking toward the door again. We were all alone in the small café, except for two women working the front counter. Chance looked around, not looking at me, then added, "It's just a mystery. We may never completely figure it out."

"It's so funny. How can you look at the world, in all its diversity, and not believe we have a creator? Let's talk about butterflies for a minute. There are nearly 18,000 different species of butterflies. Every species is different. They are different sizes, colors, and shapes. That is enough evidence for an intelligent creator, but my God went a step further. Every wing on every butterfly that has ever existed is different, just like our fingerprints. It's overwhelming to think He did that for us."

"Don't cry, sweetheart," he said, reaching across the table for my hand.

"Then I think of snowflakes. It's just too much. His love screams to us through something as simple as a snowflake. Did you know that every single one of them is different? It's hard to grasp the enormous number of snowflakes that have fallen since the world was created. Every one of them is different, and if you've ever studied them, they are magnificent, absolutely breathtaking."

"Here's a napkin," he whispered. Then he asked, "Why are you crying so much?"

"This is weeping, Chance."

He moved his chair next to mine. "What's happening? I've never seen you like this."

"I have looked into the eyes of Jesus. I know you don't believe me. Holy Spirit says you will never believe me; He says it's time for me to go."

"I don't want you to go. I think I'm in love with you."

"One of the most important scriptures in the bible is found in 1st John 7:8. '*He who does not love does not know God, for God is love.*' You deny who I'm completely in love with, Chance. It could never work!"

"Maybe one day you'll see things my way. You could start going with me. Everyone is welcome at the Great Southern Humanist Society meetings."

"I cannot take any part in those meetings. I've been in heaven, Chance. God's Holy Spirit is in me. There's no denying Christ for me. Not even for you. Even though I genuinely care about you, I can't have anything to do with your Society meetings. That doesn't mean I don't care about your soul and where you will spend eternity."

"I care about you, too. When I think about the future, I see us together. We are married, happy, and have a couple of kids. Even though I don't believe in God, I still want normal things."

"God said in Deuteronomy, '*Today I have given you a choice between life and death, success and disaster.*' God wanted us to love Him and obey His commandments. In Proverbs, it says, '*Death and life are in the power of the tongue.*' Do you know that scientific experiments have proven these scriptures?"

"No, I didn't," he replied, looking over his shoulder as the door opened.

"We determine the outcome of our lives by our choices, our words."

"I'm picking my words as carefully as I can," he almost whispered, watching the young couple sitting down near us.

"Even more than your words, where do you give your time, your money? What you believe in is like a rudder for your life. Birds of a feather... yes. But Chance, if you would only study birds and ask them for their wisdom, they would tell you the Lord's hand made them, the Lord's breath gave them life."

Chance leaned toward me, pushing back the hair on the side of my face. He whispered in my ear, "Maybe we should change the subject. Looks like we've got an audience."

"What if you were talking about your Atheist club?"

"There's no need to make a scene. I got it," he said, standing up, pushing his chair under the table.

"Are you folks okay?" The waitress asked, picking up the straw wrappers and napkins from our table.

Chance pulled his shoulders back. "Yes, thank you. We were about to leave."

"I'm not ashamed of the gospel of Jesus Christ. I will live and proclaim the marvelous works of God all the days of my life!"

"Me too. Very few people talk about Jesus these days, unless you're in a church," the waitress said, smiling. "Let us know if we can get anything else for y'all."

"Thanks," Chance said, looking at the door again.

"It feels like whatever's beyond that door is more important than what we're discussing."

"No, I'm just feeling like after we walk out that door, I may never see you again," he said, putting his hands in his pants pockets.

"Why wouldn't we see each other?"

"Because you are refusing my proposal."

"Did you propose to me?"

The chair made a strange noise as he pushed it further in. Turning slightly away from the other couple, he said, "I might have if the conversation had gone differently."

Clasping my hands over my face, I closed my eyes and sighed. The next words to come out of my mouth had to be right. I asked the Holy Spirit to help me.

"What are you doing, Kessum?"

"I'm thinking," I said, never opening my eyes.

"It looks like you're praying."

"Why does that upset you? You know who I am and what I've been through."

"Yes, I know what you have been through, and that's exactly why I want to be around to take care of you. With your injuries, you'll need someone to help you in the future."

"God is my helper. He will provide. I'm not afraid of being alone, of being a widow."

"You are not a widow. You and Shane were never married! What are you even talking about? Can't this conversation be about me and you? About our future?"

"I know I'm not a widow, but I still feel like one. Shane and I committed ourselves to each other in every way. The only thing we didn't do was make it to the altar, but we felt like we were already married in our hearts."

"But you didn't make it to the altar," Chance said, rubbing his temples.

"It's hard for me to say this. I do love you, but we do not have a future together. I've got to go," I said, picking up my purse before standing up.

"Yeah, it's time to go," he said, walking to the door.

He held the door. I walked through, stopping near the car to search for sunglasses. We stood silently, watching a car pass. I looked back at the Greenhouse and saw our reflection in the window. If anyone had seen us, they would think… what a beautiful couple. He's tall, strong, handsome, and she's pretty, with strawberry blonde hair blowing in the wind. They would never know the heaviness of our conversation or the sadness I felt.

He reached for my hand, pulling me close, saying, "Don't let this be goodbye. You never know what the future can bring. It could be you who changes my mind."

"That's the thing about God. If you're drowning, he'll send a raft. If you don't take it, he'll send a boat, and if you don't get on the boat, he'll send a ship. If you don't get on board the ship, what you decide to do next is your choice. He'll never force you to do anything, especially believe in Him."

"I'm not letting you go. I'm staying here until you say you'll marry me."

"Chance, you need to be you. I need to be me. You don't want to let me go because you can feel His Holy Spirit."

"I feel something I've never felt with anyone else, but I don't think it's that. Holy Spirit - even the name gives me chills. Isn't that part of the cross thing the Catholics do?"

"Yes, He's part of the trinity. It's not only Catholics who believe in Him. He is our comforter, our guide, sent here for believers after Jesus went to heaven."

Chance let go, stepping back before saying, "You got a spirit guiding you?"

"It's not like that, Chance. You look at everything I say the way a worldly person would see it. You have to see spiritual things as spiritual. If you can't, you won't see it. The Spirit of God is light. Without the light, you live in darkness. He is the rivers of living water that flow from our innermost being."

"You know, most religions teach you stuff to control you?"

Pressing the button on my key fob to release the lock, I stepped toward the car. My eyes filled to the brim with tears. He couldn't see them because they were hidden behind dark sunglasses. My heart felt broken. Not for the loss of a boyfriend or our future together, but for the fact that I promised Jesus I would tell them about Him. I never thought about how it would feel when people rejected Him."

"Let me get the door," he said, walking around the car.

"I've got it, thank you."

Chance stood between me and the open car door. Leaning down, he asked, "Are you the raft, the boat, or the ship?"

"I may have been all three," I said, reaching for the door handle.

"If there is a God, that's exactly how He'd be, three strikes you're out."

"It's okay, Chance, it was just a metaphor. I was trying to explain Him in terms you could understand. The truth is... He is beyond our understanding. His ways are not our ways."

"Why are you crying again?"

"Because when you leave this place, this planet we call Earth, you will have to give an account of your life. That account, the way you lived, will determine where you spend eternity. Hell is worse than anything you can imagine. Heaven is better than anything you can imagine. I'm crying because I understand we're not promised another day. We have to live each day as though it were our last, and with our next breath we will have to give an account to our Father in heaven."

"How can it be with our next breath if you're dead?"

"Heaven is more real than Earth. You are more alive there than here," I said, leaning back, letting go of the door handle.

"Kessum, you are the most beautiful woman, inside and out, I've ever known. I hate losing you, but I think you may be right. There's a huge gap between your beliefs and mine. Short of my going to heaven or hell and coming back, I can't ever see myself being a Christian. Well, maybe if Jesus came to see me like so many people claim He does. What a bunch of whack jobs."

Words of arrogance and ignorance pierced the very heart beating in my chest. How someone like him, an intelligent person, could deny our creator left me speechless. Even though Chance meant it another way, it felt like he had sucker punched me in the gut, inadvertently calling me a whack job because of what I'd shared with him.

"Jesus said, '*Whatever you do to one of the least of these brothers and sisters of mine, you have done it to me.*'"

He stepped back, with a disgusted look on his face. Then, without an apology or another word, he said, "Have a good life."

He shut the car door. I pushed the ignition button but hesitated before putting it in drive. In my rear-view mirror, I watched Chance get in his car and speed off in the opposite direction.

Without warning, an emotional tsunami began welling up from the pit of my stomach. It felt like at any moment it would reach my throat. If I allowed it to do that, it would go into my mind, and its only release would be through my eyes. I had to find some way to hold it at bay. I needed to find somewhere nearby to gather my thoughts and pray for peace. Then I remembered

Linda lives just a few blocks away, so I put the car in drive and pulled away from the curb.

CHAPTER THIRTEEN

Everything felt like it was moving in slow motion. What did I expect when Chance asked to meet? I was foolish to think we could find common ground. Something deep inside me longed to convince him that God was real. The desire never wavered, no matter what he said or believed. If he hadn't been so kind after my accident, I would have let him go. I would have released him to continue down his darkened path without another word about the immense love of Jesus. However, it was the memories of hell that pressed me to tell my testimony one more time.

Putting the car in park, I looked out my window towards Linda's front door. There was no way for me to know whether she was at home. It didn't matter. What was I going to say to her? Still, I managed to keep my emotions in check while I waited for her to answer the phone.

"Hey."

"Hey, Kessum. I was just thinking about you."

"Are you home?"

"Not right now. Are you okay?"

"Yes, no, actually, I just met Chance at the Greenhouse Cafe."

"I love that place. They have the best biscuits!"

"Yes, the food is great."

"Don't cry, Kessum. It will be okay, sweet girl."

"Not this time. He can't understand how I feel about…"

"Where are you? I'm coming to get you."

"I'm parked in front of your house. I didn't want to drive."

"It's going to take me a few minutes to get there. You're welcome to go in and make yourself at home. There's an extra key underneath that big green frog sitting on the steps."

"Okay, how long do you think it'll take?"

"About 20 minutes, but seriously, go on in. Get yourself something to drink. There's sweet tea in the fridge or soda in the pantry."

"Thanks, Linda."

We said goodbye, and suddenly, I felt a heaviness pressing down on me that I couldn't explain. I hadn't felt anything close to it since Shane died. This time, it was different. A man I love and care about isn't dead. He left because I love God. He left because he doesn't believe in God. It was easy to realize the best thing was for us to part ways. If not for the matter of his eternal soul, it would be easier to walk away. Why did I feel like a failure because of Chance's beliefs?

Linda was so gracious to offer her home, but I decided to sit in the car and wait. She was a good friend. There aren't many people I can call who would drop everything and help me.

After seeing the books about our lives in heaven, I know we were meant to meet each other. Every day, I thank the Lord that

I joined her Bible study group. If there was anything I felt confident about on this Earth, it was our divinely appointed friendship. The age difference meant nothing to us. She felt like an older sister, one I always dreamed of having when I was younger.

Thinking about Linda helped keep my mind off Chance. The last thing I wanted was to see Linda and become too emotional for words. My eyes closed as I began to pray, asking for peace. A single tear fell as my voice strained. My eyes opened to a blue jay flying past my windshield, landing on a nearby tree branch. I listened to his song, and any uneasiness I felt suddenly left.

I heard in my spirit that Linda has wisdom. I started thinking about the many stories she shared with me. Her wisdom came from years of attending church and studying the Bible.

For a moment, I closed my eyes. The memory was so clear in my mind. Jesus, sitting on that big rock near the water's edge. Then I could see myself walking toward Him. His arms stretched wide to hug me. His embrace, like a sea of love, encircled me. It went through me, healing every hurt, every wound I'd ever had. In my mind, I could hear Him saying my name. I'll never understand how I was worthy of the King of Kings to speak my name. Still, He spoke it out loud, and it felt like all of heaven listened.

The garage door lifted from the ground, and I opened my eyes. Linda pulled up beside me, waving. For a moment, I didn't want to leave the car. The peace most humans crave surrounded me like a soft blanket. When these moments happened, I only wanted to stay still and savor every last second of His presence.

In a couple of minutes, Linda stood outside my door, tapping softly on the window. I looked up to see her face, concerned but trying to look happy. Raising my index finger, I gave myself a few seconds. Putting my phone in my purse, I unbuckled the seatbelt while glancing at the mirror. Now, all I wanted was to be home praying, but it was too late.

"What happened?" she asked, wrapping her arms around me.

"He wouldn't listen," I answered, walking with her into the garage.

She opened the door, flipping the light switch. "Sometimes there's nothing we can say. People have their minds made up, and that's that. Jesus said in Matthew 13 … *'I speak to them in parables, because seeing, they see not, and hearing, they hear not, neither do they understand.'* It's hard, but sometimes they can't hear the truth."

We walked into the kitchen. Linda opened the refrigerator for a pitcher of tea. Opening a cabinet, she took out two clear glasses decorated with tiny blue flowers. After filling them halfway with ice, she poured tea into the glasses, setting one in front of me. Without thinking, I picked up the glass and drank nearly every drop. She smiled, filled it almost to the brim again, then put the pitcher back in the fridge.

"Do you want to sit out by the pool?"

Looking past the kitchen table into the living room, I nodded yes. The kitchen felt homey, but the living room was too formal for comfort. I knew the backyard was Linda's labor of love.

The moment you walked into her little oasis, you could see it had become an extension of her. The plants, flowers, and manicured grass, along with beautiful pottery and ornamental statues surrounding the sitting areas and paths, spoke to her dedication. We walked along the pebble-lined walkway, which wound through a small flower garden to the left and a grassy patch on the right, until we sat under an arbor covered with jasmine vines.

"Aww, it's been quite a week already. I'm thankful you called and got me out of that meeting."

With hesitation and a lack of anything better to say, I said, "Sorry."

"No, seriously, I didn't want to be there anyway. The church is having a few issues involving the children's ministry. They wanted my input even though I'm no longer involved."

"I guess I want the same thing," I said, watching a hummingbird hover at a feeder.

"They are just marvelous little creatures. I love watching them. Do you know they flap their wings between 40 and 80 times a second? A second! Only God!"

"Linda, why do you think Jesus sent me back?"

"You told me He wanted you to tell everyone about heaven."

"I don't think anyone is listening."

She turned toward me, reached out her hand to touch mine, and said, "I heard you, Kessum. I think more people have listened than you realize. Remember what you told me? The sea of people Jesus showed you. He wouldn't have shown you unless it could happen."

Taking my hand from under hers, I put it back on top of her hand. "That was one of the things I thought I hadn't shared. Please don't tell anyone."

"I won't, don't worry," she said, leaning back, gazing out across the pool.

"It's a mystery. The reason He allowed me to see those things in heaven."

"I don't know what to tell you. He's God, we're not."

"You got that right," I said, looking across the pool, mesmerized by the blue water.

Linda walked over to the shed, retrieved the clippers, and snipped one yellow Gerber daisy. Then she cut two dying flowers, dropping them behind the leaves. With a slight bow, she presented the flower to me before sitting back down.

"Do you want to talk about what happened with Chance?"

"He asked me to meet him. I didn't know why. He told me he's falling in love with me. He even talked about marriage."

She set the clippers on the ground, near her feet. The silence grew heavier by the second before she asked, "Is that why you're upset?"

"No. It's the choices. Sometimes they are so hard, and I don't know if I'm choosing the right ones. I feel so... ugh."

"Here," Linda said, getting up, "I think I have some..." Linda disappeared into the shed. She held the box near my hand until I pulled out a tissue, then set the box on the small table between us.

"He kept saying he wanted to be in my life, he missed me, but I told him no. I can't be in a relationship with him or a marriage."

"Kessum, he's an atheist, and he's actively encouraging other people not to believe in God. I know you care about him, but you did the right thing. Oil and water do not mix."

"I know. I was thinking before you got here; light and darkness don't mix. They have nothing in common."

Linda seemed to be in deep thought before asking, "You know it's not your responsibility to change his mind?"

"I did everything I could to convince him that God is real. He thinks that when I fell down the stairs, I was hallucinating about heaven."

"Yep! That sounds exactly like something he'd say. Now, don't get me wrong. He's a nice guy and pretty good-looking, but I don't believe God would want you to marry someone who doesn't believe in Him."

"That's exactly why I'm upset. Hell is just as real as heaven. People like Chance, who've been deceived into believing God is not real and doesn't exist, are some of the souls who populate hell. Linda, hell is worse than I can put into words. The evil, the torture that goes on and on without end."

"I'm so sorry, my friend. I can feel your pain. I wish there were something I could…"

"Pray for him. I'm sorry, it's like the floodgate opened," I said, taking another tissue.

She took a tissue, wiping her eyes, saying, "I will pray. And I'll put him on the prayer list at church. We've seen greater miracles than an atheist converted to Christianity."

"He suggested I go to his atheist meetings. Can you believe that?"

"No, I cannot! But wait, maybe that's not such a bad idea now that I think about it. Maybe we could go together."

"Linda, that's one of the worst ideas you've ever had."

"I'm not being serious, but you know what the Bible says about our adversary? He prowls like a roaring lion, looking for someone to devour."

"Like a lion, but not the lion."

Linda paused, drank some tea, and said, "I know it's hard, because people like you and me want to gather everyone together and bring them to Jesus."

"Yes, and Jesus said, '*My sheep hear My voice, and I know them, and they follow Me.*' But it still hurts."

Linda knelt on one knee, looking up before saying, "Because you loved him."

Her eyes were full of compassion, and her typically styled brown hair was a bit untidy. I reached for her hand, saying, "I only wanted Chance to be saved. It's what Jesus asked me to do."

"I know," she replied, gently squeezing my hand before standing up.

"He wanted me to become an atheist. He said that over a quarter of the people in this country don't believe in God. He said religion is just a way to control people."

"I know, there are a lot of people who think that way," she said, sitting back down.

"Then he kept talking about marriage. He said he wants me in his life. One minute, nothing but love, the next, he was shaming me, almost making fun of me because I'm a Christian."

Linda stood up and walked over to the edge of the pool. Then she raised her hands towards the sky, leaving them raised for a minute or so. Never saying a word, she lowered her arms, then sat beside me again.

"Kessum, if I remember correctly, Jesus didn't ask you to save anyone. He's the only one who can do that. He asked you to write a book. Now, I'll try to be incredibly careful here because I don't want to move you in any particular direction. When someone is in a close relationship with God, He gives them His Spirit. This Spirit is a guide, helping to lead you down the right paths in life. Without hesitation, I can tell you that if you are with Him and He is with you, you'll know when you meet your husband. Then, when he proposes, there might be tears, but they'll be tears of joy. Not the kind of tears I see on your cheeks today."

"I don't even know how to begin writing a book."

"All of this talking, and she says I don't know how to write." Linda looked at me, laughed, then said, "When you ask Him to help you, He will. He'll give you the words. I promise."

When I was back home, alone in my room, I began to pray. It didn't take long before a calming peace filled my childhood room. In the past, this room had been a place for anger, jealousy, pain, and hatred. Today, it was a place of healing, harmony, and love.

My head moved closer to the floor as I continued praying, seeking the Lord. The air around me became electric, and I knew angels were with me. My eyes did not open as I worshipped Him. With a flash of white light that I could only see in my mind, I was there.

In front of me, the ever-glowing green grass blew gently in the wind. Life was pulsating with the song of heaven, which never ceased. I wanted to run, to glide across the light shooting up from the grass. Everything within me wanted to find the living water, to see Jesus.

This time, I couldn't move. My feet were planted like a great oak with deep roots. The desire to enter heaven became overwhelming. As I twisted to break loose, I became aware of the darkness behind me. Looking over my shoulder, I realized I stood between heaven and hell. The deep chasm terrified my soul.

Turning back, my eyes scanned the field of glory for Jesus. He wasn't there, but still, I could feel Him. I looked over my shoulder. People were attempting to crawl up the sides of the dark opening. When they saw me looking at them, they pleaded with me. 'Help me! Get me out of here! I don't belong here!'

With a loud voice, I screamed, "Jesus, help me!"

The presence in the room was heavy. I rolled over onto my back, staring up at the ceiling. Tears ran down the side of my face, wetting the carpet. Then I heard a knock.

"Are you okay in there?"

"Yes, Dad," I answered, attempting to sit up.

"Your mom heard you yell. I'm just checking," he said, twisting the doorknob.

"It's locked, Dad, but I'll be out in a few minutes."

Feeling exhausted, I stayed on the floor reliving the vision. It felt like I was stuck between heaven and hell. Jesus was there. It was the same field we were in when I went to heaven, but I couldn't see Him. Then all the people in the darkness were asking for my help.

My mind was racing, trying to figure out what it all meant. I closed my eyes, saying out loud, "I don't understand, Jesus."

There was no one in the room. No one was at the door. There was just a small voice coming from my heart. I didn't hear it with my ears. It felt like my soul was the only part of me that could hear the voice. It told me that one day I would understand. I prayed that day would come soon.

CHAPTER FOURTEEN

Trina and I were invited to go boating with Cooley and a few friends. He recently bought a new boat, and island hopping was how he wanted to get her in saltwater. We were surprised to see Tommy and Sarah onboard. They recently married after years and years of dating, and they were still deeply in love. Cooley had a new love in his life, Samantha. She was tall, skinny, and very blonde. They were cute, like two teenagers who couldn't keep their hands off each other. Another couple on board were Samantha's sister Penelope and her boyfriend, Davis. Penelope's nickname was Penny, and since Davis didn't like his name, Penny nicknamed him C.K., which stood for Calvin Klein. She explained he was obsessed with the designer, and she thought guys with initial names were hot.

Trina and I were the only single ones in the group. We were the couple who wasn't a couple, but we'd been friends so long that it was okay. She recently broke off her engagement with an older guy, an investment banker whom I'd never met. She was still nursing a broken heart, so island hopping in the Gulf of Mexico was a good distraction.

Time, in its never-ending forward motion, had passed quickly since we'd all been together. It didn't take long before it felt like we'd never been apart. Cooley, Tommy, Sarah, Trina, and I fell right back into the groove and began to feel more like high schoolers rather than young adults. Samatha, Penny, and Davis were a little younger than us, but in no time, they felt like people we'd known for years.

It was a sunny day during the last days of May, and as we glided across the water's surface, it felt like summer had already begun. The water sparkled like a thousand diamonds floating upon its surface. After dropping the anchor off Horn Island, we left the boat to sit on the beach. My eyes searched up and down the water for any sign of dolphins. Out of the many times I'd been here, there were only a couple of times I hadn't spotted a few near the shoreline. We all stood on the shore searching for signs of dolphins before boarding the boat again.

When Captain Cooley said it was time to go, C.K. pointed to the west. Three or four dolphins were swimming towards us, but not too close. One fin, two fins, one going down and another fin coming up. I silently thanked God for letting us see them.

One by one, we climbed aboard. Cooley started the engine, and we took off, riding with the sun almost directly overhead. With little shade on the boat, I had to take advantage of the Bimini top to avoid getting sunburnt. Trina sat right beside me, along with Samantha and her sister. Tommy, Sarah, and C.K. sat in the sun, Sarah's hair whipping in every direction from the wind.

After thirty minutes, we spotted Ship Island in the distance. Boats dotted the shore from one end to the other. Most of them anchored near where the island's tourists gathered. Everyone who grew up on the Mississippi Gulf Coast knew that if you wanted to swim in the Gulf, you had to get to the other side of the barrier islands. The water becomes clearer, making it safer for all types of water sports. Today, the water was perfect, with soft waves. The water was still cool but not too cool to swim in. With the sun shining and very few clouds, we couldn't have asked for a better day to go boating.

Cooley idled the boat down as we reached the eastern side of Ship Island. Memories of Fort Massachusetts filled my mind, along with the many trips over the years to the island. We waved at every boat we passed on our way to the western side. Most of the people were strangers, but a few boats had old friends from school as captains or passengers. Other people who said hello, calling Cooley by name, were friends and acquaintances he knew from around Biloxi.

When we reached the opposite end of the island, I was surprised when Cooley accelerated the boat. Ship Island was one of the islands we planned to visit, and I wondered why he didn't stop. Then I realized we were going to Cat Island, my favorite island in the Mississippi Gulf.

We dropped anchor off the beach, near the center of Cat Island. Cooley gave orders to everyone just like a boat captain would. Each person had to do their part. The guys carried the heavy stuff like ice chests, chairs, and a canopy for shade. The girls brought the towels, blankets, and a picnic basket filled with plates, napkins, and cups.

The eight of us setting up for a picnic was organized chaos. Though Cooley barked the orders onboard, Trina took over on shore. In all situations, given the chance, she could make sense of chaos and turn something crazy into something peaceful. It had always been a gift she had had since we were young. It didn't take long, and everything was ready. Then the guys started gathering driftwood for a fire.

Trina and I walked down to the water to look for shells when they started cooking. Four other boats were anchored along the shoreline, but only two families were on the beach. We walked along the shore with the sun to our backs, into the wind. Her long legs slowed down to my pace. With each step, I waited for her to break the silence.

"Maybe we should go back," Trina said, stopping to look behind us. Her long blonde hair covered half her face. She pushed it back, looking at me for an answer.

We had covered a long shoreline distance, and I didn't want to stop walking. It felt like the right thing to do was to go back and help prepare lunch, but today, I didn't feel like being responsible. I wanted to be free. I felt like running down the beach. I felt like singing, screaming, or doing anything to express my freedom.

"Earth to Kessum," she roared, then laughed.

"Yes, we should probably go help with lunch. It's just so nice out here," I said, taking a few more steps.

"We can keep walking if you want. I'm sure they'll make it without us."

"Are you hungry?"

She pulled her sunglasses down her nose, moving closer to my face, asking, "Is that really a question?"

We laughed and turned back. The sun beamed down on our bodies as I realized I probably needed more sunscreen. Trina opened her bag like she was reading my mind, handing me a bottle. We stopped for a few minutes, helping each other apply some to our backs.

"What do you think of Cooley's new girlfriend?" Trina asked as though she were hiring the girl for a job.

"She seems nice enough. I can tell he likes her."

"I thought you two would be together by now. He's always liked you since, what, fifth grade?"

"Humm…" I squeezed her arm gently, saying, "He tried, a little, but it was awkward. Then he was with Tammy, and I was spending time with Chance. We both have awful timing, or it's just Jesus' way of letting us figure out we're better off as friends."

"But he tried? I'm going to need you to elaborate on that," Trina said, making a funny face with wide-open eyes.

"He's just a little flirty and hanging on a little too long when we hug."

"I think you're blushing, Ms. Howards. Oh my goodness! After all these years, you still have a crush on your first boyfriend."

"Come on, Trina. You know, I could never be with Cooley after Shane. It just wouldn't feel right, but I've always liked him. He's… well, he's cool. You know him."

"Yes, I know him, and yes, he's cool. Alright, next subject. How's it been going since you moved?"

"I like having my own place, but it gets lonely sometimes. I got used to Mom and Dad being around every day."

Trina didn't respond. She stopped, watched the waves before asking, "What about Chance? Do you ever see him?"

"No, I haven't seen Chance in over two years. The last time we met was at the Greenhouse in Biloxi. We're still friends on Facebook. He's engaged to a girl with a five-year-old daughter from New Orleans."

"It's hard to imagine him being a stepdad. I hope that woman knows what she's getting herself into."

"I think he'll be a good dad. He always talked about having children," I said, stopping to look out into the Gulf.

"Things are going to work out for you, Kessum. Me too! One day, we'll have engagement parties, weddings, and receptions. Then it'll be baby showers and our kids' birthday parties, and don't forget anniversaries. Our husbands will buy us the most expensive, extravagant gifts! Yep! That's going to be us. And our kids will grow up together. Our families will go on vacation together twice a year. In the summer, we'll go to the beach, and in the winter, we'll go to the mountains."

"I believe everything you just said because that's God's plan for my life. I will be married and have two healthy children, and my husband will be a good, Godly man."

"Are you still going to church?" Trina asked, looking over her shoulder back toward the canopy.

I looked in the same direction, adding, "Looks like they've got the fire going, and yes, I am going to church. What about you?"

"I need to get back in the habit of going. It's just I go out on Saturday night and stay up too late to make it on Sunday morning," she replied, picking up a shell, throwing it in the water.

"There are churches having services at other times, like Wednesday night, Sunday night, even a few on Saturday. I'd love to say you can get everything you need by attending church. Unfortunately, it doesn't happen, but going to church helps. Ultimately, it's you, God, Jesus, and the Holy Spirit. Nobody can create or maintain your relationship. Still, church is important, but it's not everything."

"I'm still a little confused about the Holy Spirit. I wasn't raised in a church that talked about it," Trina said, then picked up a piece of driftwood and started drawing a heart in the sand.

"Holy Spirit isn't an 'it.' He's a person. He's my best friend. My everything."

"Please, I didn't mean to upset you," she said, dropping the stick and putting her arm around me. The height difference had always made me feel like Trina was older than me.

"You didn't. Sometimes, when I talk about Him, I get emotional. If only everyone on Earth knew and loved Him and listened to Him. He's so kind, Trina."

"Are you going to write about what happened to you in Heaven?"

I thought about what she asked, then put my sunglasses on my head so she could see my eyes. "Do you remember that song, I Can Only Imagine, by Mercy Me?"

"Yes! I love that song," she said, taking my hand and squeezing it.

Tears stung my eyes. "I don't have to imagine. All I have to do is close my eyes, and I'm there, in the arms of Jesus. You can try to imagine, Trina, but you can't. Take every person, every single minute you've ever felt loved, and times it by a billion, and maybe it would come close to the love I felt when He held me in His arms. Jesus is love, and His love is the purest, most amazing thing I've ever felt."

"You're right, it's hard to imagine, but when you talk about it, I feel something. It's hard to describe. Kind of like… I'm excited, or happy, full of anticipation. It makes me feel better," Trina said, putting her sunglasses on her head to look at me.

"Heaven is more real than this place. When you're there, God is everywhere. It's hard to describe Him, but the space He fills with the light of glory is enormous. He's in everything; He is everything. The music is Him and the angels! Oh, Trina, the angels. They're so beautiful, full of light, and so powerful. When I feel afraid, I think about the angels guarding me until I go back home."

Trina looked puzzled, tilting her head toward the sky before asking, "Back home?"

"This place is not our home. When Jesus said he went to prepare a place for us, He meant it. Heaven is our home, and I know I'm going back there one day soon."

"It must feel good to know that, to have that kind of reassurance of going to heaven. One day I think I'm saved and the next, I know I'm headed straight for hell," she motioned, with her thumb pointing down.

We stood side by side, arms around each other. I said, "Trina, God loves you so much. He loves you more than you can comprehend. He has a plan for your life. All you have to do is believe Jesus is the Son of God. He came to Earth and died in your place so you could be reconciled with God. Tell Jesus you want Him. Tell Him you give Him your life. He'll always be with you."

Trina whispered, "I believe in You, Jesus. I know You died for me. I give You my life. I love you so much. Please never leave me."

"He'll never leave you. Let me pray for you, Father, forgive Trina for all her sins. Wash her clean and set her free. Fill her with your Holy Spirit, for Him to help and guide her throughout the days of her life. In Jesus' name I pray. Amen."

We embraced, shedding only a few tears, and then burst into laughter. Then we started walking back down the beach. She looked unsure but waited for me to speak.

"Oh, I almost forgot to tell you. I've already started the book. But as you know, I'm not a writer. You're the one who helped me with all my book reports in school."

"Yes, but everything is different now. After losing Shane, having your accident, going to heaven, then falling in love with an atheist, you've changed just a little bit," Trina said, holding her thumb and index finger close together.

"Yes, I have. Even though it hasn't been easy, I think it has changed for the better."

"I agree. Not that you were bad before, but you were a little hotheaded. A tiny firecracker, not a big one."

"You are too funny! I don't think you have room to talk."

"Can you hear Cooley?" she asked, putting her hand behind her ear.

"Goodness, why is he yelling so loudly?"

"Must be getting close to time to eat," she said, grabbing my hand. We ran toward the canopy, holding hands like young schoolgirls would do.

Trina looked different, happier. Samatha and Sarah noticed and asked what had happened on our walk. When Trina didn't explain, neither did I. We just looked at each other and giggled like we did back in high school when we had a secret.

With our plates full of food, we sat side by side, hoping to escape the hot afternoon sun. Cooley was like an amateur comedian, doing his best to make us laugh. When he told one that was a little inappropriate, Samantha elbowed him. She looked straight at me, shrugging her shoulders.

"That's almost PG for Cooley-O! You should have heard the ones he used to crack in high school. It's a wonder he didn't get kicked out after our English teacher overheard him that one day," Tommy said.

"Hey, that teacher loved my jokes! I was her favorite student," Cooley replied, standing up to flex his muscles.

C.K. stood up, saying, "If we're flexing, I'm in."

"That's unnecessary," Penny said as Tommy joined them.

Samantha sighed before saying, "Look at these big, strong men, girls. Those arms, those legs! With all that strength, we won't have to carry a thing back to the boat except ourselves."

Penny interrupted Trina, saying, "I think they are flexing so hard that they should carry us, too!"

Trina said, "That's exactly what I was going to say."

"Great minds think alike," Samantha said, high-fiving Penny and then Trina.

"You girls got it all wrong," Cooley blurted out. "Yes, we could carry y'all back to the boat. That wouldn't be a problem, but God made all of you to be man's helper, not man's back breaker."

"You are so hilarious, Sir Cooley-O," Samatha yelled, fake laughing.

"Well, I may be hilarious, but I'm your only ride out of here. I think you need to be a little sweeter to the captain," he said, standing to give a salute.

"He's right," Tommy replied. "It's a long swim back to Gulfport."

Cooley added, "Yes, it is, and we're going to catch the sunset on Ship Island. There's a whole group of people meeting us. It's going to be funnnn!"

"I'm ready; let's get packed up," Trina said, taking her last bite of strawberry.

"As soon as everybody's done, we'll get going," Cooley said. He looked at me, winked, and took another bite of his sausage dog. Mustard fell on his chest, and then he grunted. His girl-friend used her napkin to wipe it off. She looked at him with love, and I felt they would probably be married before we started decorating Christmas trees.

It was late afternoon before we loaded the boat and headed back to Ship Island. It was a short trip, but Trina and I still sat where the sun couldn't reach us. When we reached the western side, Cooley eased off the throttle. Then, he surprised everyone by letting Samatha steer the boat to the other end of the island.

Cooley directed her to where the other boats were anchored before he took over. Trina and I sat still, waiting for the guys to throw the anchor in the water. Three boats sat on our right side and four or five on the left. Some people stayed on their boats while others waded in the shallow water.

The beach in front of the Ship Island store was full of tourists. At least fifty blue umbrellas shaded over one hundred guests. Children were playing and swimming, but only a few adults were in the water. The lifeguards scanned the beach, keeping a close eye on everyone.

As soon as the boat stopped moving, I climbed down the ladder and jumped into the water, walking ashore. Samantha asked if I wanted company, and I nodded, telling her to join me. Sarah kissed Tommy and jumped in, hurrying through the salty water to catch up. It was my first chance to go to a real bathroom since this morning, and I wasn't waiting around.

After our trip to the bathroom, we stopped by the store to buy candy and ring floats. I didn't want the other girls to feel left out, so I got one for them, too. The lady behind the cash register offered to inflate them, so we walked with her to the side of the building. There was one red, two pink, one green, and one blue float, but it didn't take long before they were ready.

Samantha wore a pink float around her waist. I carried the other pink and red ones on one arm. Sarah had the other two, one around each arm. We rushed across the long, hot boardwalk toward the beach. I thought that when we reached the sand, it would give us a little relief from the heat, but the sand felt almost as hot as the boardwalk.

A strong breeze came out of nowhere, sending a float off Sarah's arm up into the air. She yelled and then ran down the beach after it. The wind sent it sailing out past the breaking waves, and for a moment, it looked like it was lost forever.

Then I saw a guy sitting on his boat watching us. He stood up, diving into the water like he was an Olympic swimmer. I began to wonder if he would ever break the surface, then something strange happened. If I hadn't seen it with my own eyes, there's no way I would have believed it. He was swimming, but still a reasonable distance away. The wind picked up the float, and it dropped almost right in front of him. If the man hadn't come up for air, he might have swum right past it.

He hooked the float around his arm and swam on his side with the other arm until he could touch bottom. We stood watching, cheering him on as he pushed his tan body through the water. As he got closer, I could see a tinge of red in his cheeks. He looked right at me and smiled. I felt my heart skip a beat.

"Thank you," Sarah said, walking into the water to meet him.

"You're welcome," he replied, his light blue eyes twinkling in the afternoon sun. He held out the blue ring-float in front of him, giving it to Sarah.

"You're our hero, thanks," Samantha said with a sweet southern drawl.

"I didn't want one of you ladies to be without a float," he said, looking back at our boat. "Cooley told me to meet him here around sunset."

"Well, that doesn't surprise me. I don't think we've met before. I'm Samantha, Cooley's girlfriend," she said, introducing herself while extending her hand.

He shook her hand, smiled, then looked at me, saying, "And this is his…"

"This is Kessum, an old friend of his. They went to school together since second grade. And this is their friend Sarah, who also went to school with Cooley."

"Very nice to meet y'all. My brother Mike and his girlfriend, Angela, are still out there," he said, pointing to his boat.

"What's your name?"

He laughed, looked away, then introduced himself, "I'm Craig, Craig Phillips. And you're Kessum. I've never heard that name before."

"It's original; my dad will have to explain it to you one day. That's if you ever meet my dad."

"Awkward," Samantha said, covering her mouth with her hand.

"I was trying to explain that my dad made up my name. He says I am one of a kind. I deserve a one-of-a-kind name," I said, through uncontrollable giggles.

"Well, Craig, Craig Phillips, thanks again for saving our float. I guess we'll see you later," Samatha replied, tugging my shirt.

After nodding, he turned back toward his boat, took a few steps, and dove into the water. I stood still, watching him swim, as the other girls walked further into the water, sitting on their floats. I waded out to them when Craig was almost back to his boat. I didn't want him to catch me watching him.

When we got back to the boat, Cooley put a rope through the floats. Then he tied them to the chain on the anchor so we wouldn't float away. After applying more sunscreen, we ate candy before we got in the water to float. It wasn't long before several other couples joined us, and we had a little crowd.

As the sun sank deeper into the western sky, evening colors emerged—shades of blue, red, orange, pink, and purple—coloring our incredible view. With the tourists gone, almost everybody left their boats and went ashore. Some people walked the shoreline, others spread blankets on the sand, and a few brought chairs.

Cooley lay across a blanket, rolling over to look at the sky. Samantha sat down beside him, and Penny sat beside her. Trina took her beach towel by the corners, raising it in the air, then laid it on the sand. Tommy and Sarah walked hand in hand along the shore. I took my towel farther up the beach to put it on drier sand.

"Are you too good to sit with us?" C.K. asked.

"No, I'm right here. I just wanted to be a little farther from the water. I'm feeling a little chilly since the sun is going down."

Craig emerged from the water, asking, "You want this towel? We could both sit on yours." Craig offered, wrapping his towel around my shoulders and using another to dry his body.

"Sure, thanks," I replied, heart racing, scooting over.

He wrapped the other towel around his waist before sitting down. "Looks like you got a little too much sun."

"I did. Along with this hair color comes lighter skin," I said, holding my hair out.

"What color is your hair?"

"My Mom says it's strawberry-blonde. Your hair is like mine; it's not brown, but it's not blonde."

"It's brown but gets lighter in the sun."

"So it's going to change even more before the end of summer," I replied, touching his hair.

"It's not as soft as yours," he whispered, studying me with his eyes, touching the hair falling over my shoulder.

I turned slightly, looking at his face, asking, "Are you from Mississippi?"

"Not exactly. I've lived here since I was twelve, but we moved over from Louisiana."

"What part of Louisiana?"

"We moved from Metairie, just outside of New Orleans."

"Yes, I've been there. It's been a while," I said, thinking about how close he was sitting next to me.

He shifted, then turned his head, saying, "Maybe we could go there one day. There's so much to do there, and New Orleans is just a short drive."

"That would be fun."

"Tell me something," Craig said.

I noticed his white teeth even in the softer light of sunset. I asked, "What do you want to know?"

"I want to know about you. What do you do? What do you like to do? What do you want to do with your life?"

We locked eyes, and for a moment, I wasn't sure how to answer him or which question to answer first. Craig moved again, and his arm touched mine. My heart raced, and I struggled to find words. "Umm… can you repeat the questions?"

"Let's start with the first one. What do you do?"

"At the present, I'm not employed, if that's what you're asking. Well, I am working, but not for a paycheck. I volunteer at a nursing home. I visit, play games, or help in any way I can. I'm also involved at my church and attempting to write a book."

"Attempting… I can't imagine a girl like you attempting to do anything. What's your book about?"

"It's about God, Jesus, and Holy Spirit, heaven, and a little about hell."

"Okay. Tackling the big subjects right off the bat. You're in the big leagues, don't even need a warm-up book," Craig said, swinging an imaginary bat.

Looking toward the sunset, I replied, "I guess I don't."

"Jesus is one of my favorite subjects. I can't wait to read it."

Surprised by his response, I answered, "Okay, I'll give you a copy when it's published."

"That'll work! I know this is strange, but I feel like I've known you for a long time. Have you ever felt like that before? Meet somebody and feel like you already know them."

"I kind of feel that way right now."

He moved a little closer, accidentally pulling the towel off my shoulder. "I'm sorry. Here, let me…"

"It's okay, I'm feeling warmer now."

Craig reached around, gently pulling the towel down off my other shoulder. We leaned closer, our eyes locked, and suddenly, my world became blurry except for him. It had been so long since a man's lips touched mine. I closed my eyes, waiting, full of anticipation. I could feel his breath as he leaned even closer. We kissed… a soft, gentle kiss, and then he moved, leaning back.

The voice I came to know and love spoke to me. The voice I could only hear in my heart and soul gave me a gift. It was one of the greatest gifts of words I'd ever heard. No one could hear those words except for me. Not Craig, Trina, or even my Aunt May, who had been in heaven for years.

Holy Spirit said, '*My daughter, this is My son, your husband. He will care for you all the days of your life.*'

"I didn't mean to make you cry," Craig said, wiping a tear from my cheek with his fingertip.

"It wasn't you; I just heard something when we kissed," I said, reaching for his hand.

"You heard Him, too?" He asked, hesitating before saying, "He told me you're His daughter."

"Yes, I am."

He stood up, reaching out his hand, asking, "Do you feel like walking down the beach?"

"Yes, that sounds good," I said, taking his hand.

We walked past all our friends and his brother. They were talking, but we were in our own little world. The sun was nearing the water as he took my hand. When we touched, it felt like electricity flowed from his body into mine.

I tried to speak, but my mind was not clear. As we walked hand in hand, I closed my eyes. I saw a vision of heaven. Jesus was on His White horse, and I was on mine. In the distance, a beautiful blonde-headed young girl came riding up, dressed in white. Sitting behind her was the cutest brown-haired boy I've ever seen. I opened my eyes and realized the little boy looked like my future husband.

Praying silently, I thought, 'Thank you, Father, for giving me my life and a future. Jesus, I miss You. I miss being in heaven with You, but now I understand why You sent me back. Help me fulfill my purpose and love people the way You love them. Holy Spirit, thank You for guiding me and always giving me comfort. Stay with me all the days of my life, giving me the words to lead others into a relationship with You. In the holy, mighty name of Jesus, I pray, believing You hear my prayers and answer them. Amen.'

The Gift

What can I give Him,

Poor as I am?

If I were a shepherd

I would bring Him a lamb,

If I were a Wise Man

I would do my part, -

Yet what can I give Him,

Give my heart.

Christina Rossetti

Dear Reader,

Thank you for reading *Kessum*. This story was born from a deep place in my heart—a place that has known brokenness, longed for healing, and ultimately has been transformed by His love.

The story of Kessum reflects what happens when we lay our pain, the past, and the future at the feet of Jesus and allow Him to love us. I pray that as you walked with Kessum through her trials, revelations, and redemption, you saw pieces of your own story and came away with a renewed sense of purpose, peace, and belonging.

Jesus sees you. He knows you. You are loved more than you can comprehend. And like Kessum, you were created for His glory.

With all my heart,

Charna Ainsworth

ABOUT THE AUTHOR

Charna Ainsworth is a Christian author, poet, and photographer known for her heartfelt, faith-centered stories and inspirational poetry. Drawing on her Southern roots and deep personal faith, Charna writes to uplift, heal, and point readers to the love of Jesus. Her works explore themes of redemption, grace, and supernatural encounters with God. She is the author of *The Mountain of God, Unlikely Christian, I Will Adore You, Rivers of Living Water,* and the visionary novel *Kessum* —a moving tale of transformation set against the backdrop of Heaven's glory. Charna lives in Mississippi with her family and continues to create works that shine light into darkness and encourage readers to walk boldly in their divine calling.

Please visit: www.charnaainsworth.com

www.kessum.com

Reviews are welcome and appreciated. Links to multiple book venues are listed below.

Amazon:

https://www.amazon.com/author/charnaainsworth

Barnes & Noble:

https://www.barnesandnoble.com/s/Charna%20Ainsworth

Apple Books:

https://books.apple.com/us/author/charna-ainsworth/id543148723

Also By Charna Ainsworth

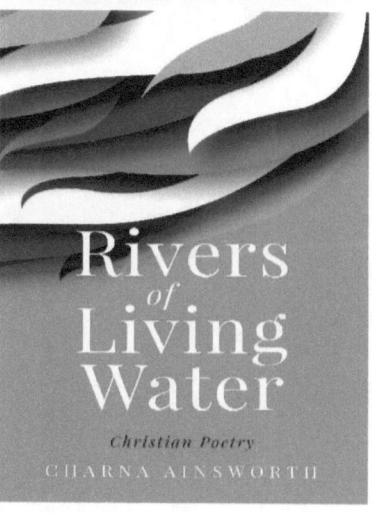

www.ingramcontent.com/pod-product-compliance
Lightning Source LLC
Chambersburg PA
CBHW020756250626
47155CB00003B/1108